The Champion
of Merrimack County

The Champion of Merrimack County

Roger W. Drury

ILLUSTRATED BY FRITZ WEGNER

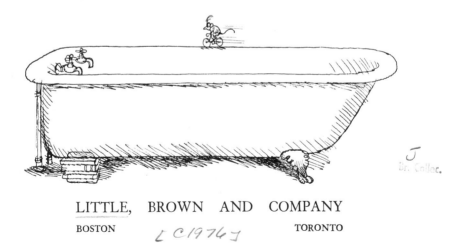

LITTLE, BROWN AND COMPANY

BOSTON   [C 1976]   TORONTO

FIRST EDITION

T 10/76

Library of Congress Cataloging in Publication Data

Drury, Roger Wolcott, 1914–
  The champion of Merrimack County.

  SUMMARY: The discovery of a bike-riding mouse in
the bathtub is just the beginning of a series of
humorous complications for the Berryfield family.
  [1. Mice—Fiction] I. Wegner, Fritz. II. Title.
PZ7.D838Ch   [Fic]   76–6453
ISBN 0–316–19349–6 ✓

Published simultaneously in Canada
by Little, Brown & Company (Canada) Limited

PRINTED IN THE UNITED STATES OF AMERICA

The Champion
of Merrimack County

1

"I DON'T BELIEVE IT," whispered Mrs. Berry-field. "In your father's new bathtub! On a bicycle! I simply don't believe it!"

Mrs. Berryfield and Janet sat down on their heels on the bathroom floor and gazed over the side of the tub.

"It's only a little bicycle, Mom. There's plenty of room."

"I know. I know. But in the new tub! You heard what Daddy said when he left for work this morning — It can't be true! How do you suppose it ever got down in there?"

"I think it's a 'he.' That's a boy's bike. Maybe he was riding around the edge and fell in."

Mrs. Berryfield shivered.

"Look how steep it is," she said. "He could have broken a leg. He could have tangled his tail. He could have smashed his bicycle to smithereens."

O Crispin pretended not to hear them. He was used to

being watched and talked about. Since March he had been practicing for the State Bicycle Rodeo on every kind of track he could find — rough ones, smooth ones, hilly ones, flat ones — and Mr. Berryfield's new bathtub was by far the best of them all. It was so convenient, too, just upstairs from the cellar where O Crispin and his family lived.

None of the other houses in Bel-Air Park had cellars. They were modern, flat-roofed, one-story structures, built on concrete slabs. Until last fall the Berryfield house had been like that too, but Mr. Berryfield had kept saying it was pathetic for a house to have no cellar or attic. He said the bathroom was no bigger than a closet, and the bathtub was so short that a man had to fold himself up like a capital W to get into it. And that wasn't all! The sides of the tub were so low that you couldn't wiggle your toes without splashing water on the floor.

He had put up with the house and the bathtub for the twelve years that he and Mrs. Berryfield had lived in Bel-Air Park. Twelve years was long enough! At last he had saved money to build a small wing. It stuck out from the side of the house, making the bathroom twice as big as before. In the end of the new bathroom was a stairway down to a small cellar underneath, and another stairway up to a second-story attic above.

Mrs. Berryfield thought it would be terribly inconvenient going through the bathroom on the way to the attic or the cellar, but she didn't tell him so. Nor did Janet tell him that some of her friends were saying the enlarged Berryfield house looked like a camel. Mr. Berryfield was an important man in town. He was Research Director of the Merrimack Playground Equipment Company and he wasn't used to being told anything.

The new bathroom was certainly big enough for the kind of bathtub he wanted, but most of his weekends for two months had been spent writing letters and making telephone calls, before he located just last week what he called a "proper tub."

The man who sold it to him said he could guarantee it was a genuine antique. Mr. Berryfield said anyone could tell that by looking at it. But he didn't mind. It was a proper tub and that was what mattered.

Enormous and white, it stood in the middle of the room, supported on three short cast-iron legs shaped like lions' feet, and a pile of paperback mystery stories where the fourth leg should have been but wasn't. It was long enough for a tall man

like Mr. Berryfield to stretch out in — all six feet, two inches
of him — at the end of his day's work; and it was so deep,
he told Janet, that water wouldn't go over the side, even when

you snoozed in it, with everything under except your face.

The steep sides curved at the top into a smoothly rounded rim all around. Outside one end, hot and cold water pipes rose straight through the floor, each with its own handle and a spout overhanging the tub. A chain with a dangling rubber drain plug was looped over one of the spouts.

It was a splendid tub, and from the moment he first laid eyes on it Mr. Berryfield loved it dearly.

Janet and her mother now sat on their heels beside this marvelous tub and watched. Janet couldn't bear to look away from the bicycle and rider as they went round and round. Nothing so exciting had ever happened in the Berryfield house before. She wanted it to go on and on. But it would have to be a secret.

She had never had any kind of pet, unless you counted the woolly bear caterpillar her father had consented to let her keep in a jar last winter. He said the house was too small for pets. Fathers and mothers usually had to take care of them, and the kind that ran loose in the house, he said flatly, were a menace. You never knew where they might be next.

Janet looked at her mother.

"Do we have to tell Daddy about this?" she whispered.

Mrs. Berryfield stared into the tub.

"It can't be true," she said. "I don't believe it. It just isn't sensible."

Of course, she had known all along that having an attic and a cellar would lead to trouble — rubbish, dirt, who knew what else? About Christmastime it had begun: nibbling in the kitchen, scratching and hurrying noises in the walls. Mr. Berryfield had said "Pooh! It's not as bad as you think!" He would build her a mousetrap when he got around to it.

Weeks went by. Then, during his first bath in the new tub, he had heard a crash in the cellar. Something had knocked a can of nails off one of his shelves! Immediately, everything was different. Mice in *his* workshop? It was an outrage!

"I won't stand for it!" he stormed. "I didn't get this new tub so they could turn my shop upside down while I'm snoozing. Don't you worry! I'll clear them out!"

Right after supper that evening, he had gone down to his carpentry shop in the cellar and begun to make a mousetrap, inventing it as he went along. By the time it was put together, baited, and set, the next evening, the front hall clock was striking midnight.

"Never mind if it's late," he had told her as they settled down in bed. "I intend to put a stop to this nonsense before it goes any further."

On Sunday morning he had been all scowls. The cheese was gone and the trap was empty. The same thing happened the next night. And the next. He assured Mrs. Berryfield there was nothing wrong with the trap. All it needed was a little adjusting. But the adjustments he made didn't help. The trap was robbed five nights in a row.

This morning, he had been almost too angry to speak.

"All right," he had said, as he stamped out of the house to go to work. "If they won't get caught in my trap, just wait till I come home today! They're going to wish they weren't so smart!"

Now, kneeling with Janet beside the tub, Mrs. Berryfield remembered his threatening look and words.

"Oh dear!" she said.

"What is it, Mom? Sore knees again?"

"No, it's not my knees. Well, yes, my knees are hurting, but I meant — if your father got so angry hearing mice in his workshop, what will he think about this?"

O Crispin paid little attention to the two soft voices. He was busy, and he was happy — too happy to worry about the dreadful plans of Mr. Berryfield — because he had discovered a new racetrack, the most beautiful racetrack he had ever seen.

Round and round the bottom of the tub he went, with his

chin cocked up so the breeze would tickle the curls of short, wiry hair along his throat.

No one else in the family had hair like that. Because of it, his mother and father had named him Crispin when he was born. They said it was a sign he would become famous, but they had never dreamed he would be Champion of Merrimack County!

His other name, O, was nothing special. Each of his brothers and sisters had been given a letter of the alphabet too. His letter was O because he was the fifteenth to be born, and O was the fifteenth letter. Nowadays, when he raced, he used both names, O Crispin. It sounded like a winner's cheer and was easy for the crowds to yell as he flashed by.

Every time he came to the foot of Mr. Berryfield's tub, he steered within a squeak of the drain hole and ducked his head going under the dangling rubber plug. At the other end there was nothing in the way and he could pedal faster. The extra speed carried him in a little swoop up the slope as he went around. The sensation was delicious, like being a stone whirled on the end of a string. Never had he seen such a smooth, beautiful place to ride a bicycle.

He looked up and saw, above the white walls, the faces of Mrs. Berryfield and Janet still intently watching him.

"Now," he said to himself, "now I'll show them why the crowds go wild when I pass the stands. I'll show them what it means to be the top mouse of Merrimack County."

He gripped the handlebars, leaned forward, and pumped his sinewy legs up and down. The bicycle raced along the floor of the bathtub. Turning the sharp corners, right and left of the drain hole, the tires screeched, the handlebars trembled, and it was all he could do to hold the front wheel steady.

Each time around, he swung the bike further up the curving ends. With his chin almost touching the handlebars, and his tail hooked over one shoulder to keep it out of harm's way, he threw every last pinweight of energy into the whirling pedals.

Once, his speed took him higher at the end of the tub than he expected, so that he swung breathlessly down and had to cross the bottom at an angle when he was halfway to the other end. What luck! He soon discovered he could get extra speed this way, by steering his bicycle in a figure-eight course instead of an oval.

Faster and faster he went. He sailed up the head slope nearly to the top, then plunged like a rocket towards the drain. Once, twice, three times, and then, next time around — whoosh! his bicycle climbed all the way to the rim of the tub at the head end, with speed to spare.

"Yow!" yelled Janet. "He made it!"

Mrs. Berryfield gasped and clapped her hand to her open mouth.

"Watch out!" she cried. "Watch out, little mouse! You'll go over the edge!"

O Crispin threw her a scornful glance as he squeezed the brakes and took the first corner on the sides of his tires.

"Over the edge, indeed!" he muttered. Just the same, he did have to be careful. Riding on the rim of the tub was like riding along a pipe. If he wavered from the center, he might go off altogether. Pedaling as fast as he dared, he made two sizzling trips around, with his nose in the air.

"Does she think I'm a beginner? If she got a fright out

of that, wait till she sees my 'Rolling Down to Rio'!"

He slowed his bike to a stop at the middle of the head end, and looked down the long white slope to the floor of the tub. It was the loveliest sight he had ever seen. He had coasted down it once already, and what a run it had been! But he wouldn't coast this time. Not he, the prize racer of Merrimack County! Not with onlookers! This time, he would do it wide open.

He pointed the bicycle straight for the drain hole, adjusted the chin strap of his electric-blue crash helmet, set his right foot on the pedal, and shoved off.

Mrs. Berryfield shrieked, "He'll kill himself!" Janet gulped and dug her fingers into her knees.

Down plunged O Crispin, pedaling like a demon, aiming along his nose at the plug hanging from the water spout.

Janet went suddenly cold all over. When she had used the tub before breakfast, there had been a thin bit of soap stuck on the bottom — all that was left of a cake that had slid into her father's bath last evening. It was still there, white on the white tub, almost invisible, squarely in the bicycle's path.

She wanted to warn the mouse, but her voice froze in her throat. The next few instants seemed to her a dreadful eternity.

O Crispin had swerved and avoided the soap on his first run this morning. But this time he was going much faster, and he had forgotten the soap was there. He was almost on it, going like a rocket, when he judged the time had come to cut speed.

"Rio Grande!" he yelled, and gripped both handbrakes at once.

Janet mistook his cry of triumph for a squeak of terror. She hoped the soap was dry.

It wasn't.

The front wheel cut into it and began to slide. The back wheel followed and began to slither. Lurching wildly, the bicycle shot ahead. O Crispin kicked out with his feet, first left, then right, to keep his balance — and then, CRASH! both wheels skidded suddenly from under him and down he went, bicycle and rider shooting helplessly towards the drain.

There was a screech, as one pedal scraped along the bottom. It caught in the drain, flinging the bicycle violently around, and the front wheel slammed and crumpled against the end of the tub.

An instant later, the mouse slid, BANG! into the wrecked bicycle.

2

KEEPING BOTH EYES SHUT, as he always did when he first woke up, O Crispin lay still and listened. Two voices were talking — a young one and an older one.

"He's breathing," said the young voice. "I'm positive he is. I saw his whiskers move. I hope he hasn't broken anything."

"Anybody can see his front wheel is broken," said the older voice.

"Oh, yes," said the first, "but that's not his."

"You don't mean to say it was a *borrowed* bicycle?"

"Oh, I hope not," said the young voice. "Poor mouse! No, I meant it's not part of him, like his arms and legs. How can we find out if those are all right?"

O Crispin lay still, wondering what the two voices were talking about. What mouse? What bicycle? What were people doing in his bedroom?

Something hard pressed on his shoulder. His tail ached. He opened one eye a crack. Was that a bicycle wheel lying on top of him? No, it seemed to be a whole bicycle. He shut his eye again and tried to think. Why was there a bicycle in bed with him? It must be a dream. He opened his eye again. The bicycle was still there.

"It was all because of the soap," said the young voice. "His wheels were in it when he put on the brakes."

"But even without the soap," said the other voice, "even without the soap, do you think he could have stopped? It's not sensible. How could anybody expect to go tearing down a hill like that and not crash into the other end — or fall down the drain? This mouse is either crazy or else he's a real daredevil."

"He's a special mouse," said the young voice. "That's what he is."

Ah! Now O Crispin remembered who and where he was! Indeed he was a special mouse! The youngest champion Merrimack County had ever had! He had found a racetrack which was white; smooth as glass. He was showing off that stunt no other mouse could do, his own stunt, the "Rolling Down to Rio." But he had never tried it on so steep a slope before, and something must have gone wrong, because here he was now, flat on the ground, with his bicycle on top of him.

"I must have made a fool of myself," he thought. "In front of onlookers. Me, the Champion of Merrimack County!"

Just to think about it made him ache all over. He wished he were at home in the cellar. He was afraid he was going to cry.

The two voices began again.

"Mommy, look!"

"Yes, I see. Poor thing! If that's how he feels, he'll want to be by himself. And anyway, Janet, it's time for you and me to go and make our lunch."

"And decide what to do about him," said the young voice, "and about his bike."

O Crispin heard Janet and Mrs. Berryfield tiptoe away.

"That lady," he said to himself, "the old one, she's sensible, like my mother. She does scare too easily, but she knows when a mouse needs to be alone."

He tried his arms and legs, one by one. They were stiff, but they didn't hurt when he moved them. He opened and shut his mouth and ran his tongue over his dry lips. He took several deep breaths, then opened both eyes and looked as far as he could without turning his head, right and left, up and down.

So far, everything worked.

"Nothing wrong with me," he thought, "except that I behaved like a booby." He grasped the bicycle by its frame, lifted it aside, rolled over and got on his feet.

OW–W–W–W! What was that thumping ache out behind?

Holding his tail still, he turned around to look. Sure enough, his beautiful, smoothly-tapering tail had a lump in it.

"It looks as if I had swallowed a peanut whole," he thought, "and it had gone down part way into my tail and stuck there."

But it was no joke. Suppose the tail was broken. The last time a member of his family had a broken tail was when his grandfather G Rufus had walked in his sleep to get away from an imaginary cat and backed into a real mousetrap. The whole family, including Grandpa, had been awakened by his howls of pain. They had pried him loose with a nail. But the broken tail took weeks to heal and never could be curled into neat spirals again. The best Grandpa could do after the accident, by great effort, was to whip it into a sort of clumsy question mark. And it ached on rainy days.

The more O Crispin thought about his grandfather, the more his own tail hurt. How could he avoid meeting people while it healed, having to explain what had happened — and having to admit what a booby he had been? How would he be able to manage it on a bicycle?

The bicycle! What kind of champion was he, not looking first to see if his bicycle had been damaged?

Oh disaster! The front wheel was ruined beyond repair! And he, the Champion of Merrimack County, was supposed to wear the county colors at the State Bicycle Rodeo only three days from now! It was too much.

He crept to the end of the tub, dragging his aching tail, sat down under the plug with his back against the cold white wall, took off his crash helmet and held it in his lap, and stared at the red cockade he had won in his last big race.

Here he was, down in this slippery racetrack, with a wrecked bicycle and a broken tail. On top of that, didn't he remember one of those voices saying that something terrible would happen "when Daddy comes home today"?

3

JANET RAN ALL THE WAY to Harry's Bicycle Shop, two blocks down the hill from the gate of Bel-Air Park.

The worn-out asphalt sidewalk on the hill was an old friend, full of freakish cracks, whiskery with grass. Its surface had waves like water, bulging up and down and never quite the way her feet expected it to be. It was twice as much fun as the smooth new sidewalk in Bel-Air Park.

Harry was an old friend too. Like the sidewalk to his shop, he was full of twists and surprises that made it fun to visit him. And he understood about pets. Janet had been to the bicycle shop every day of this April vacation to see the five newborn beagle puppies in a carton in Harry's back room. But she wasn't thinking about beagle puppies today.

Harry was bent over a new bike, polishing it. Since he didn't see her come in, she stood silently just inside the door, catching her breath and wondering how she would ask for a wheel for a mouse's bicycle.

When she and Mrs. Berryfield had looked in the bathtub after lunch, they had found the mouse fast asleep under the hanging drain plug, with his swollen tail stretched out beside him. They had thought about nothing else during lunch, discussing what to do, and had agreed on one thing. This amazing mouse must be saved from whatever Mr. Berryfield might be planning.

But when they returned to the bathroom, they had been dismayed to notice for the first time the dark line scratched by the mouse's pedal along the bottom of the tub when the bicycle had crashed. Janet ran her fingers across it, hoping it might rub off. But it was no use. The white enamel had been scraped off down to the metal beneath. She and Mrs. Berryfield looked at each other, not needing to say a word. They both thought, "Daddy can't help seeing that; and how will we explain?"

Mr. Berryfield would be home from work in about five hours. If he discovered his precious tub had been used for a racetrack — by a mouse — that would be the end! It would do no good to remind him that he had let the cake of soap fall into his bath. He would never admit the accident had been his fault. It wouldn't help to tell him that the mouse was hurt. He would say, "A mouse is a mouse."

"If it was any other mouse," Mrs. Berryfield said to Janet, "I'd have to agree with him."

"But it isn't any other mouse," Janet had said. "It's this mouse. We just have to take care of him and his front wheel and that awful scratch before Daddy comes. We have to!"

Mrs. Berryfield felt the scratch again.

"It's really there," she said. "But I still don't believe it. Why did it have to happen in this bathtub? It isn't sensible! Whatever will we do?"

Janet saw very clearly what to do.

"I'll go down to Harry's and get a new front wheel," she said. "I have three dollars and ten cents. That ought to be enough for a wheel this size. While I'm doing that, you can take him to the doctor and get his tail fixed."

It had been easy enough to say, but now that Janet was here at Harry's shop it didn't seem at all easy to do.

Harry hung his rag over the rear fender of the machine he was at work on, and looked up at her.

"Hi, there!" he said. "The pups have been squealing, 'Where's Jan?' all morning. Aren't you going to— Hey! why so quiet? Vacation ending? Is that it?"

Janet swallowed.

"Do you have pieces of bicycles?" she asked. "I mean, can a person buy a front wheel all by itself, or do I have to get a whole bicycle?"

"I sell parts, sure; that's no problem," Harry said. He picked up the rag and wiped his hands. "Is it a wheel you need? Were you trying to knock over a tree?"

"It's not my bike," Janet explained. "Mine is all right. It's a — a visitor's bike."

"Same size as yours?"

"Oh no. Smaller."

"You don't know the size?"

"Not exactly. I brought the bicycle with me, so as to be sure."

"Good girl," said Harry. "That makes it easy. You left it outside?" He went towards the door.

"No," Janet called after him. "It's here."

Harry turned to see her reaching into her jeans pocket. He scratched his head.

"Roomy jeans they're making nowadays! How much of it have you got in there?"

Janet pulled out a little bundle with an elastic band around it. As she took off the elastic and started to unwind the tissue paper wrapping, Harry's smile faded.

"She's kidding you, Harry," he murmured. "She's pulling your leg. She's tweaking your spokes!"

"There!" said Janet. The last of the paper came off, and the mouse's bicycle lay in the palm of her hand, plain to see. She held it out to him.

"Well, bless my old Aunt Alice's seven-toed cat! Where'd you get this?" Harry gently picked up the tiny machine and

examined it, first one side, then the other. "Let me try something," he said.

Leading the way to his workbench, he took down a slender tool and flicked the edge of one of the pedals. It whirled noiselessly, on and on, until finally it slowed to a stop.

"Look at that!" Harry exclaimed. "Couldn't be ball bearings in there. It's just too small. But golly, did you see it go?" He held the tiny bicycle under his workbench light and studied it again.

"That chain — impossible! Pick me a purple buttercup, Jan, if it hasn't even got gears! Wait a minute; let me see if this works too." He found a pair of tweezers and very carefully squeezed the black bulb of a horn attached to the handlebars.

"Hear anything?" he said.

"No. Did you?"

"No. Maybe I should have squeezed it more suddenly. Listen!"

This time they both heard a thin squeal — about halfway between a yelp and no sound at all.

"Like a pup in a rabbit hole!" Harry laughed. He gazed at the bicycle admiringly. "And to think it's all not much bigger than my thumb! But that front wheel — it makes me sick to look at it. What happened?"

Pictures began to flash through Janet's memory.

"Well, you see," she began, "he skidded in the bottom of the tub and banged into the end under the faucets." With a dreadful, hollow sensation in her stomach, she remembered how the mouse and bicycle had looked, sprawled motionless after the crash.

"It's just lucky he didn't kill himself," she added.

"If you ask me," said Harry, "he shouldn't have been allowed to take a beautiful thing like this into the tub with him in the first place. This belongs in a museum. What did he want to do? See if it would float?"

"Oh no, he was riding it."

"Riding it?" Harry stared at her. "In the bathtub?"

"There wasn't any water in the tub. Didn't I tell you?"

Harry's glance wandered from the bicycle in his hand to Janet, and back again. With the tip of one finger on the seat, he balanced the tiny machine upright in his palm.

"All right," he said. "Let's begin again. He was riding it in the bathtub. Now tell me, Jan Berryfield, and tell me slowly, because my wits are all of a wobble: *who* was riding this bicycle in the bathtub?"

4

"A MOUSE?" cried Harry. "Riding this? In your bathtub? Look me in the eye, Jan Berryfield, so I can see if you're smiling."

Janet scowled at him.

"I *only* told you about the mouse," she said, "because you asked me. And I don't care if you believe me or not, so long as you have a new wheel to put on, in place of the busted one."

Harry scratched his ear.

"You expect me to carry spare parts for a bike that size?"

"Well, this is a bicycle shop."

"Yes, but—"

"And that's a bicycle."

Harry brought the little machine on his open palm up to the level of his chin, and considered it for a moment before replying.

"Sure it's a bicycle, but fly me to Spain on a bumblebee if any customer of mine ever used this size. Until your mouse. And him I haven't seen, only heard about. Look over there." Harry indicated a rack of wheels on the wall behind the counter. "See the littlest ones? Those are back wheels for tricycles. They don't come any smaller than that."

"But I have to get a new wheel for this, somehow. I absolutely have to. Quickly — this afternoon."

"Golly, Jan!" Harry shook his head. "It could be made, I suppose; but I don't know about this afternoon. And offhand I can't think of anyone who's in the mouse bicycle business. It's more like a job for a — for a—" He paused and began to smile. The smile spread over his whole face. "Y' know, I've got an idea! Hey! Have I ever got an idea! You say you're in a rush? Here!" He thrust the mouse's bicycle into Janet's hand. "Bundle this up again, quick, while I write a note to leave on the door."

By the time Janet had the little bicycle safely tucked in her pocket, Harry was beckoning her to hurry along. Out of his back room he wheeled a long red and black bicycle, with two seats, two handlebars, two sets of pedals, and a deep wire basket over the front fender.

"I'll take the front seat," he said. "You hop on behind and help make the wheels hum. Leave the steering to me."

"But where are we going?" Janet finally found breath to say, as they swung out into the street. "And what for?"

"Wheels!" shouted Harry. "A dealer in wheels! Little wheels! Lots of them! Just what you need!"

They rode down to the river, along the embankment, over the bridge and past a dreary row of old brick mills — all empty now except for the one used by the Merrimack Playground Equipment Company. As they turned into a narrow street in the oldest part of the city, an ambulance raced by, its siren howling, "wow-ee, wow-ee, wow-ee," and Janet began wondering if Mrs. Berryfield had found a doctor to take care of the mouse's tail. It would do no good to mend the bicycle if the mouse couldn't ride it. Where would one put a broken tail to keep it out of the way? What if it slipped down and got caught in the back wheel? Ouch! The very idea made Janet's insides ache.

"Stop pedaling!" Harry commanded suddenly over his shoulder. "We've arrived!"

The bicycle halted with a long groan of its brakes, in front of a shop which, Janet saw, had a clock face painted on the inside of its window. Above the clock hung a sign, lettered in dusty gold, "SILVESTER PYE, CLOCKMAKER." Suspended from the E of PYE, a long brass pendulum hung down behind the painted clock, as motionless as if it, too, were painted there.

"In you go," said Harry. "No time for gawking." As he pushed open the screen door, he sang out, "Arise and shine, Great-Uncle Silvester. It's Thursday afternoon and I'll bet you a pint of scrambled watchworks your pendulum hasn't been wound all week!"

A stooped, smiling, little gnome of a man, with white hair over his ears and a watchmaker's magnifier in one eye, half fell off the tall stool behind the counter and went to the window.

"You're right," he murmured. "It's not even ticking. Disgraceful! Disgraceful! You should come and remind me more often." He wound a spring on the back of the sign, then pushed the pendulum over to one side and let it go. For the first few swings, it made a great commotion, jerking the sign this way and that and threatening to pull the whole contraption off its hooks. Then it settled down to a steady, squeaky ticking, to and fro, and Silvester Pye returned to his stool.

Harry was holding out his hand, palm up, as if he expected something. The aged clockmaker looked blankly at the hand, then at his own hands, which were empty. He scratched his head, took the little magnifier out of his eye and grinned sheepishly.

"You know my bad memory, Harry," he said. "Was I supposed to be fetching something for you?"

"A pint of scrambled watchworks," said Harry. "Because you let your pendulum stop."

"A pint. Oh–oh–oh–oh. Let me see. A pint. Would that be the same as half a gallon?"

"Half a quart," Janet said.

"Half a quart? Yes, of course! Half a quart. Thank you, young lady. Thank you. It's confusing." The old man smiled vaguely. "Half a quart of what was it?"

"Watchworks," said Harry. "Scrambled watchworks."

"Scrambled watchworks! Well, isn't that lucky! I happen to have at least a gallon on hand." Silvester Pye opened a glass-fronted case on the wall. On the bottom shelf was a row of paper cups, one of which he carefully lifted out. "There! Did you say half a pint?" He looked earnestly into the cup, jostling it back and forth.

"Pretty well mixed, I think," he said; "but I can jumble it more, if you like." He set the cup down on the counter.

"Thanks," said Harry. "It's muddled enough already, I'm sure. Now, Jan, how does this look to you?" He tipped the cup and poured out on the counter a glittering huddle of little steel screws, brass rods and pins, steel springs, and especially wheels, both brass and steel. A few were large as a quarter; others were the size of nickels, and a great many smaller than a dime. Some had solid centers. Some were open-work, with wide braces joining their centers to their rims.

"Wheels!" gasped Janet. "Look at them all!"

She dug her hand into her pocket, brought out the bundled-up bicycle, and began unwrapping it.

Silvester Pye was sympathetic when he saw how carefully she had bound it up.

"A broken watch, is it?" he murmured. "How well I remember when my first watch got broken!" But as the last of the tissue paper came off, he saw that this couldn't be a watch. He looked to Harry for help.

"What is it the young lady has there, eh?"

"What do you think it is, Uncle?"

Mr. Pye put the little magnifier back in his eye and stared.

"Well, it looks like a bicycle. But how did it get so small? What happened to it?"

"An accident in her bathtub."

"In her bathtub? And it shrank that much?" Silvester Pye shook his head. "Isn't that shocking! I hope she didn't buy it at your store, Harry. And it needs a new front wheel. But —" Mr. Pye peered closely at the bicycle, "even if you do fix that bunged-up wheel, where will you find anybody small enough to ride it, the size it is now?"

Harry jerked a thumb at Janet, who was busily searching through the pile of watchworks on the counter.

"Friend of hers," he said.

Janet looked up at Harry unhappily. She was holding one of the bigger brass wheels.

"What are we going to do?" she said. "Here's one just the right size, but it's like all of them: it has teeth around the outside, see? The bicycle would go g-jog, g-jog, g-jog, and all the mouse's teeth would fall out."

Silvester Pye shuddered.

"Terrible, terrible!" he said. "Dentists are so expensive! But if your problem is a bumpy wheel, I can tell you the very best man in town to fix it for you."

5

MRS. BERRYFIELD hadn't needed to think twice where to go about the mouse's injured tail. She took him straight to Doctor Potts, whose office was on the ground floor of his house, only a block beyond the bicycle shop and an easy walk from Bel-Air Park.

Doctor Potts had been the family doctor ever since Janet's first year at nursery school. That year, he had taken one look at Janet's wrist, which she had sprained on a new pencil sharpener Mr. Berryfield had bought her, and then he had opened a closet in his office and pulled out the biggest roll of adhesive tape Mrs. Berryfield had ever seen.

"We will strap it up," he said, "and it'll be as good as new in no time. This sticking plaster is wonderful stuff, Mrs. Berryfield. I'm a great believer in it."

He certainly was. Sprains, pains, aches, breaks, even sore

throats (so Mr. Berryfield claimed) — whatever the ailment happened to be, Doctor Potts did it up in sticking plaster, yards of it usually, and sometimes he put a bow on top like a Christmas box — "to make it feel better," he said.

Now Mrs. Berryfield thought to herself that she had sat many times in Doctor Potts's outer office, without ever seeing a mouse waiting for an appointment. For that matter, she had never seen a fox or a kangaroo or a beaver waiting there, either. In fact, nothing with a tail.

Yet Mrs. Berryfield was sure it was no mistake to bring the mouse. Doctor Potts was a kind and gentle man. A mouse wouldn't be frightened of him, especially not a daredevil mouse like this one.

Now, as she entered the office, Doctor Potts smiled at her across his inkwell. Would he still smile, she wondered, when he discovered she had brought him a mouse for a patient? It might be best to break it to him slowly.

On the edge of his desk, between them, she set the shoebox in which she had put the mouse and half an old towel to make him comfortable. The box was still shut and tied with string. She resolved not to open it until the doctor asked her to.

"What seems to be the trouble, Mrs. Berryfield?" Doctor

Potts pulled out a clean sheet of writing paper and took the cap off his pen. "Is that shoulder of yours misbehaving again?"

Mrs. Berryfield smoothed her skirt and looked at the floor. "No, Doctor, that's been fine. I—" She stopped, looked at him and looked back at the floor. Then she began again.

"Have you ever had a patient with a swollen tail?"

Doctor Potts acted as if she had squirted him in the face with a water pistol. The pen jumped from his hand and clattered to the floor and he turned suddenly away, making a gasping sound like a potato exploding in the oven. Was he laughing? Mrs. Berryfield couldn't imagine why he should. But while he was bent over, looking for his pen, the gurgling that came from behind his desk did sound very much like a man laughing and trying not to be heard.

By the time he got back in his chair with his pen ready, the only sign of laughter on his face was a little twitch at the corner of his lips.

"Now," he said, "you asked, do I ever have a patient with a swollen tail? The answer is, yes ma'am, indeed I do! They don't come to see me about that, but I can tell you there are plenty of 'em. If that's your problem, you don't need to worry. A little exercise will cure it."

Mrs. Berryfield stared at him.

"Exercise? Oh!" She chuckled. "Then you *were* laughing. No wonder! No, Doctor, I didn't mean that kind of swollen tail — not just a fat bottom. This got hurt in a fall from a bicycle. It may be broken."

"Broken? Is walking terribly painful?"

"Oh, I am sure it is."

Doctor Potts thought this was a strange thing for her to say. Had he heard it right? Or was he going deaf? He cupped a hand behind his ear.

"What's that? You say it *is* painful?"

"Oh yes, Doctor. There's no question about it."

The doctor rubbed the cap of his pen against his lips for a moment.

"I might examine it here," he said finally, "but the very best procedure is to get an X ray, so we'll know if any bones really are broken. Then I'll do it up for you." He pushed a button on the base of his telephone.

"Winchester Hospital? Doctor Potts speaking. Please send the ambulance to my office to pick up a patient for X-ray. . . . Mrs. Dorothea Berryfield. . . . B as in blueberry. . . . That's it, Field. Use a wheelchair."

Next, he called the hospital X-ray room.

"Potts speaking," he said. "I'm sending you a patient with a possible sacroiliac fracture."

"Broken tail," interrupted Mrs. Berryfield in a loud whisper.

Doctor Potts clamped his hand over the telephone and frowned playfully at her as he hung up.

"You're not a doctor," he said, "so you can call it a broken tail, or a fractured fanny-bone, or anything else you like. But if I started using that kind of talk, they'd be gossiping up and down every corridor in the hospital, 'Have you heard? Poor old Potts is dotty.'"

"But mice do have tails, Doctor, don't they?" Mrs. Berryfield insisted.

Doctor Potts was writing again, but at her question he stopped and gazed blankly at the paper. Why the devil was she talking about mice? Or was it true that his ears were failing him? He looked up.

"Certainly. Yes indeed!" he said. "And, by the way, if this *is* a sacroiliac fracture, it will need to be handled gently. So you must promise me to ask no questions, but do exactly as the people at the hospital tell you."

"Oh I promise," she assured him. "But do you think a wheelchair and ambulance are necessary?"

"They are, Mrs. Berryfield. Absolutely." Doctor Potts regarded her with a stern face. "And you just promised to ask no questions."

The wail of an approaching siren warned her to get ready. It was really a great relief to see Doctor Potts taking the whole thing so seriously. She moved the shoebox carefully into her lap, and in a few moments two ambulance attendants brought in a wheelchair. Obediently, she allowed them to ease her into it. Doctor Potts patted her on the shoulder.

"Good luck!" he said.

As the wheelchair rolled on its rubber tires out the door, she pictured the mouse resting inside the dark shoebox, hardly knowing that he was being moved at all. She called back to Doctor Potts.

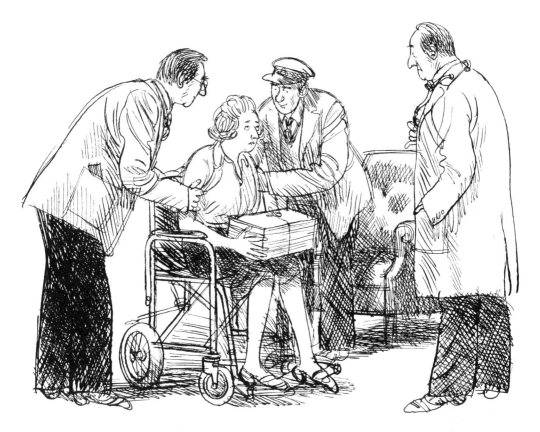

"You've been so considerate, Doctor. I'm sure it will be the most comfortable ride this little mouse ever had."

Doctor Potts stood at his window until the ambulance drove off.

"'Little mouse,'" he muttered to himself. "There's nothing wrong with my ears. I'm sure she said 'little mouse.' And all that about a broken tail! I think there's something broken in her head, poor lady." He rang the hospital X-ray room.

"Potts again," he said. "Keep a sharp eye on that Berryfield woman. She seems to believe she's a mouse."

6

"WELL, WELL, MRS. BERRYFIELD," said the X-ray nurse, with a quick, efficient smile. "We had a call from Doctor Potts and we're all ready for you. Believe it or not, this will be the first time we ever X-rayed a mouse!"

For Mrs. Berryfield it was a first time, too. She had never been to the hospital X-ray room before. They wheeled her down a long zigzag of corridors with shiny floors, and she felt as helpless as a bit of fluff pushed along by a dust mop.

"Here we are," said the nurse as they entered a room at the end. "Now we'll take off your dress and put a gown on you."

The gown turned out to be a short-sleeved muslin thing without buttons, tied by tapes at the back. It looked silly.

"But why must I get into that?" objected Mrs. Berryfield.

"Hospital rules," said the nurse. "Everyone has to. Buttons and zippers spoil the picture."

Mrs. Berryfield couldn't see why *her* buttons would hurt the *mouse's* X ray, but then she remembered her promise to ask no questions.

"It's all for the mouse's sake," she told herself. And no matter what was happening, she was careful to keep the shoebox beside her or in her hands, right side up.

A man wearing all white clothes, even white shoes, came in and looked at her curiously.

"A mouse, eh?" he said.

"That's right, Doctor," she said. "With a broken tail."

"Well, something new every day! Shall we try for a picture or two? I'm not a doctor, by the way; just the cameraman. Call me Fred. Now if you'll come over here — carefully, please! — we'll get you up on the table. You can leave your box on the chair. Miss Carpenter will take care of it for you."

Mrs. Berryfield held the shoebox tightly.

"Oh no," she protested. "I'll hold it till you're ready."

Fred winked at the nurse.

"That's all right," he said. "It won't do any harm for her to keep it."

They had Mrs. Berryfield get up carefully on the table and lie on her side. Then Fred moved a big camera, which hung from the ceiling and rolled on overhead trolleys, until it was directly above her. So far, they had said nothing about putting the mouse under the camera.

"Instead," thought Mrs. Berryfield, "they act as if they're getting ready to take an X ray of *me*." The shoebox was on the table beside her head, but the camera was in position over her hips, nowhere near the shoebox.

"There!" said the man in white. "That's just right. Now, don't move!"

Mrs. Berryfield suddenly thought, "Good heavens! Do they think it's *my* tail that's broken?"

"Wait!" she cried. "Hold on a minute! Aren't you going to X-ray the mouse?"

The nurse rested a firm hand on her shoulder.

"Of course, Mrs. Berryfield," she said. "If you'll just stay quiet for a couple of minutes, we'll have our picture of the mouse."

Mrs. Berryfield forgot everything Doctor Potts had told her about obeying the nurse. She was filled with boiling anger. The nurse had practically called her a — a—. It was outrageous! She reared up on the X-ray table, holding the shoebox protectively under one arm.

"Young woman," she declared, "I'm the mother of a ten-year-old daughter. My husband is a respected playground equipment engineer. For twelve years we have been residents of Bel-Air Park, and I am a member in good standing of the Daughters of the American Revolution. Do I look to you like a mouse?"

The nurse glanced in alarm from Mrs. Berryfield to Fred the cameraman, and back.

"Well, if you aren't a mouse," she said, "who is? And what did Doctor Potts mean?"

Mrs. Berryfield set the shoebox down on the X-ray table and slipped off the string.

"The mouse is here," she said, as she lifted the cover. "And the tail you're supposed to X-ray is his, *not mine*."

Fred pointed at the box with a trembling forefinger.

"You mean — you've got a real mouse in that?" He peered cautiously over the edge. From one of the folds of Mrs. Berryfield's old towel, the nose and whiskers of the mouse emerged, and two black, beady eyes stared up. Fred backed away. "Don't let him out of there," he begged. "How do you know his t-tail is injured?"

"Be sensible!" scoffed Mrs. Berryfield. "You know that the minute you see it. And it's obvious from the way he walks that it hurts him terribly. I'll empty him out of the box for you."

"No! Wait!" cried the nurse. She was halfway to the door.

"Is he tame? I know it sounds like a joke, but I really can't stand rats and mice. Will he stay up there on the table?"

Mrs. Berryfield slowly turned the shoebox on its side, and then a little more than that, and lifted it until the rumpled towel slid out on the table. There was no sign of the mouse. She glanced into the box.

"Must be hiding in the towel," she said. "Tame? How would I know? He's probably just a regular wild mouse." She picked up a corner of the towel. "But with a tail like that, he's not likely to go rushing around."

The towel lifted clear of the X-ray table, and there was O Crispin. His tail, with the lump in it, lay stretched out behind him and his polished helmet gleamed like a blue light above his unblinking little eyes.

"See?" said Mrs. Berryfield. But by this time both Fred and the nurse had retreated to the sides of the room.

O Crispin looked up and saw the huge X-ray camera with its stainless steel arms and trolleys. He looked down and saw his own face in the mirror-smooth, black tabletop. The thought flashed through his mind, "What a beautiful surface for a race!"

To find himself there with a broken tail and no bicycle — what a cruel disappointment it was for the Champion of Merrimack County!

What did they expect him to do, these people? He took a few painful steps toward Mrs. Berryfield, but she quickly got down off the table. The man in white was whispering to her from a little side door that opened off the X-ray room.

"Leave him right where he is; I'll get a picture." The man ducked out of sight and called, "Don't breathe! Don't move!" There was a short humming sound, and then his grinning face appeared around the door jamb and he said, "Got it! Now, if you'll *please* put him back in the box—"

To O Crispin it was all very humiliating. They were treating him like a savage from some backward country. Couldn't one of these hospital people understand how he felt and do something to make his tail stop hurting?

He looked pleadingly at the nurse. But Miss Carpenter, who was standing against the big door to the hall, had never before seen a mouse say "please." She didn't know what he might be thinking. She gripped the doorknob hard and stared back at him.

O Crispin swung his head to the man in white. Would he help? But when Fred saw O Crispin's little black gimlet eyes fixed on him, with the blue bubble of the helmet above them, his heart jumped a beat.

"I've got to get out of here!" he gasped. "It's looking at

me! It's looking at me!" He pushed the nurse aside, jerked the door open and fled in panic down the hall.

They could hear his voice going off in the distance — "There's a mouse on the X-ray table, in a blue crash helmet, with a lump in its tail. And it looked at me! Help! Help! It looked at me!"

7

A CLOCK STRUCK TWO in Silvester Pye's back room, as the old man scooped the pile of watchworks off the counter and back into their paper cup.

What? Two o'clock already? Janet realized she had left the house a whole hour ago, yet she was as far as ever from getting the bicycle mended. If she hadn't been in such a rush, it would have been fun to spend a whole afternoon watching Mr. Pye. The absentminded old man was exactly the right kind of uncle for Harry. But all she could think about now was how to make him move faster. He paid no attention to her fidgeting.

"If your problem is a wheel with bumps on it," he kept repeating in his high, wispy voice, "take it to Bangs. Bangs is the man. He's an old-time blacksmith, and an old-time blacksmith is what you need."

"For cart wheels, sure," objected Harry, "but, Uncle, this is a bicycle wheel. And look at the size of it!"

"Small it is, but still it's a wheel. Don't argue with me, Harry. Bangs is your man. We were in grade school together, he and I. Anything a blacksmith can do, he can do."

"All right, then, Uncle," said Harry, "but we'd better get the glue off our axles. At the rate we're moving, your blacksmith may go out of business before we get there. How do we find him?"

Mr. Pye threw up his hands.

"Oh!" he said. "I could never tell you how to find the place. It's way out beyond — beyond— I'll have to come and show you."

Harry looked doubtful.

"On my bicycle? I already have Jan here on the back seat."

"Then let me ride in that big basket on your handlebars."

"Remember, Uncle, we don't want any wrong turns," Harry warned. "If you scramble us the way you scramble some of the watches you take apart, we'll be pedaling around Merrimack County till the moon comes up."

Janet shuddered. It mustn't take that long. Her father mustn't get home from work before the bike was mended and the mouse bandaged, and both of them safely hidden from him.

"We can't take all day," she whispered to Harry. "The mouse may be at home already, waiting. If I don't get there soon, with the bike, I don't know what may happen to him."

Mr. Pye guided them back past the empty mills; across the big iron bridge again; through streets with wooden, two-story houses behind big old trees, on both sides; and along a crowded highway where Janet had never been before. There seemed to be nothing but filling stations, hamburg stands, bowling alleys, and used car lots, one after another.

Presently, they turned off on a narrow side road. A farmer, plowing a big field on a tractor, waved at them. After that, they made so many turns that Janet lost track of them.

The old watchmaker, with his legs dangling out of the basket, kept telling them, "now go there," or "turn right," or "now left," or "follow your nose." At some turns he was silent and seemed to be asleep, and Harry had to wake him to get directions. Once, Janet was sure they were on a road they had traveled over earlier in the opposite direction, but just when she was ready to give up hope, Mr. Pye slapped the side of the basket and pointed.

"Here it is! 'Bangs the Blacksmith'! I could have sworn he was on the other side of the road, but this is the place! See his pile of old horseshoes?"

Sure enough, a tremendous heap of rusty horseshoes shaped like a sugarloaf stood in front of the forge, at the roadside. Against the base leaned a slab of iron on which was etched, "Bangs the Blacksmith."

Nibbling at a pile of hay beside the door was a big, brown, bony, sway-backed horse, with black numbers painted on his hooves: 1 and 2 on the front hooves, 3 and 4 on the back ones. A sign hung around the animal's neck, on which was lettered the word "Samples."

An anvil stood at the other side of the door, covered with the rust of many years' disuse, and dimpled all over the top by hammer blows. It had a heavy blacksmith's hammer welded to the top at an angle, looking as if, the last time he

used it, the blacksmith had whanged it down so hard that it had stuck there for good.

A short, square man in a long leather apron came blinking out of the forge into the sun. The top of his head was bald and red as a grape, but his eyebrows made up for it, growing like two white bushes above his squinting eyes.

Was this Bangs the Blacksmith? Janet asked herself. It didn't seem that he could be old enough to have been at school with Silvester Pye. Certainly there was nothing feeble in the voice or the handshake with which he greeted them. He noticed Harry looking at the anvil.

"Pull that hammer loose," he boomed, "and I'll shoe your

horse free for nothing." He pointed at the animal beside the door. "This is Sam, my sample horse. Four styles of shoe. You can take your pick. Sam's wearing one of each."

"Slow down there, Bangs," Silvester Pye broke in. "We didn't bring you a horse to have shoes put on, but a bicycle wheel to have bumps taken off." He leaned over the side of his basket and looked down at the front wheel of Harry's machine, then at the rear wheel. "Which is it, Harry?" he said. "Didn't you say you had bumps on one of them?"

"Braid my back spokes, Uncle!" said Harry. "Don't scramble the bicycles! He's being forgetful again, Mr. Bangs; it's not this bike but another one. Belongs to the young lady's . . . friend. Front wheel got mashed. It's an odd size, but we found a wheel at Uncle's shop that ought to work, if we can get rid of the cogs — the bumps, you know, around the edge. Show it to him, Jan."

At first, when Bangs saw the wheel, he didn't say a word, but one of his bushy eyebrows lurched down, one up. Then Janet unwrapped the mouse's bicycle. Bangs rocked back on his heels and nearly fell over the anvil.

"M' gosh!" he muttered. "Who told you to bring that to an old stonefingers like me? Silvester Pye, I'll wager it was you. You should have known I don't have the hands for work so fine as that.

"If you want my advice, young lady, if you want the teeth off that wheel there, then take it to a dentist. They've got all the right tools for tinkering with teeth. My son-in-law could do it for you. He's a dentist — a good one. Yes sir, young lady, if you take your toy bike to Peter Norton, you won't be sorry."

"Will he really fix the wheel himself?" Janet asked. "And not send us somewhere else? If we keep going from one place to another like this, the whole afternoon'll be used up, and then—" She looked woefully at Harry. "What if we get lost between here and the dentist?"

"Don't worry, Miss," said the blacksmith. "You won't get lost. I'll come along on my sample horse to guide you."

Janet's spirits began to rise again as they set out for the dentist's office. Bangs led the way on Sam, and the long bicycle followed, with Harry and Janet pedaling and Silvester Pye in the basket as before.

But there never was such an easygoing horse as Sam. With the blacksmith on his back, his middle barely cleared the road. He walked, he ambled, he *plodded* along, showing no ambition to travel faster, except once when he stepped in a puddle and splashed his belly. That startled him into trotting for two or three steps. Then he settled down again to plodding on his numbered feet, one . . . two . . . three . . . four.

Following him at that slow pace, Janet and Harry could hardly keep the bicycle from tipping over.

"Hey, watch out there!" exclaimed Mr. Pye, as the wobbling of the handlebar basket shook him out of a doze. "Are you falling asleep? We almost went into the ditch."

Janet appealed to Harry.

"Couldn't we go faster?"

Harry called out to the blacksmith.

"Mr. Bangs, if your horse would like to trot for a change, we can keep up with him."

Bangs shook his head.

"No," he said. "Sam'd just as soon walk. He always walks when he's got samples on. So would you if you had four feet and a different kind of shoe on each of them. Matter of fact,

Sam walks no matter what. And it's safest, now that we're in the city."

When they reached the dentist's office, Sam was still fresh as a daisy, while Janet — full of impatience and exasperation — felt as exhausted as if she had run a mile. She rang the office bell several times as they entered.

The clock in Doctor Norton's waiting room said ten minutes past four. It was more than three hours since she had left home to get the wheel mended, and nothing was done yet! Luckily, no one else was waiting to see Doctor Norton.

Almost immediately, the office door opened and out came the dentist himself, holding his glasses in his hand, to see who was there. He looked as if he had just been washed and ironed. He was dressed in a pale blue jacket, gray trousers

gathered at the ankle by heavy elastic bands, and saddle shoes.

"Daddy Bangs!" he exclaimed, his round face lighting happily. "Have you brought me some customers?"

"Well, sort of," said the blacksmith. "My old schoolmate, Silvester Pye, and friends of his."

Doctor Norton saw the watchmaker staring at the elastics on his trouser cuffs.

"Between you and me," he explained, "those are so I won't trip on my trousers when I'm jogging. You can't imagine how numb my feet get, standing all day beside my dentist's chair. So I jog between patients, to keep them awake. The feet, not the patients. Sometimes I even have to stop and jog between teeth."

"Between teeth!" cried Harry. He pressed a hand against his jaw and groaned. "Cuddle my motherless molars, if I'd want you jogging between mine!"

Janet dug into her pocket for the mouse's wheel.

"Speaking of teeth—" she began.

Doctor Norton grinned.

"Yes," he said. "I suppose that's why you came. Which of you" — he put his glasses on and looked around — "is the patient? Or is it all of you?"

"Here," said Janet. "It's this." She handed him the watch-work wheel. "Please look at it right away. We want—"

"Wait!" Doctor Norton put a finger against her lips. "I must examine it first." He took the wheel to the window, where he stood and studied it with a magnifying glass, both sides, and round and round the rim.

"Don't rush me," he said. "I must be sure I have seen everything." After he had examined the teeth, one by one, he turned to Janet again.

"It's funny," he said. "Between you and me, I don't find anything wrong. All the teeth seem to be where they ought to be, evenly spaced, strong, and well polished." He glanced at the blacksmith. "What is it, Daddy Bangs? You're grinning like a horse. Is this another of your pranks? Like that hammer on your anvil?"

"B' golly, no," said the blacksmith. "Tell him, Miss. Tell the doctor what you wanted me to do to those teeth there."

"Cut them off," said Janet. "Make it smooth all round, so the bicycle won't go bump, bump, bump."

Doctor Norton eyed Janet out of the sides of his glasses.

"Bicycle go bump?" he said. "What on earth does this wheel have to do with a bicycle?"

It took another whole hour for Janet to explain about the mouse's accident in the Berryfield bathtub, and for the dentist to recover from his disbelief and grind off the cogs on the watchwork wheel. Janet was growing desperate.

"Let's go," she begged. "After we get home, we still have to put the tire on the new wheel and put the wheel on the mouse's bicycle."

But at the last moment, when Sam with Bangs the Blacksmith on his back, and Harry's bicycle with Harry, Janet, and Silvester Pye on it were about to set off for the Berryfield house, Doctor Norton rushed out on the sidewalk and pleaded to be allowed to join them.

"Between you and me," he said, "I've got to see that mouse on his bicycle."

"We have no room," said Harry. "There are three of us already on this machine of mine."

"And if Sam takes another passenger," added Bangs, "he'll run aground."

"Think nothing of it," said Doctor Norton with a wave of the hand. "I can jog along behind."

So off they went at last — Sam walking in front; the long bicycle wobbling at Sam's heels; and finally the well-pressed dentist jogging in the rear, very slowly so as not to trip on the bicycle.

"Please, Mr. Bangs," Janet called out, "please make Sam go as fast as he can. We have to get home before Daddy. We have to."

8

HIGH UP NEAR THE CEILING, tired, hungry, and disgusted, O Crispin crouched on the top of the X-ray camera and looked down. No one was in sight.

"They all ran like beetles," he thought. "That Fred blasted off down the hall when I only looked at him. My Mrs. Berryfield chased after him to make him hush. And the nurse — I don't know where she went. I wonder which of them'll be back first."

As it turned out, the first person to appear was none of them, but a thin woman in a white coat, carrying a large brown envelope which she was examining as she entered. Without raising her eyes, she called out commandingly, "Fred!" There was no answer. O Crispin watched her and kept still.

"Fred!" she called again. Still no answer. "Drat the man!" she said. "He's supposed to be here." She pulled an X-ray film out of the envelope, held it up to the light and gave the ghostly image a long, expert look. Then she slid the film back in the envelope and looked at the writing in the upper corner.

" 'Berryfield, Mrs. Dorothea.' 'Doctor Potts.' Humph! If it's Potts's patient, that might explain it." At the bottom of the envelope, she read, " 'Lower spine — fracture.' " She pulled out the X ray and looked at it again.

" 'Lower spine,' indeed! Potts is dotty. That's no lower spine! It's an honest-to-goodness tail, if I ever saw one. What's more, there's a whole chipmunk or something on the front end of it."

She used the wall telephone to call the reception desk.

"Has Doctor Potts come in yet? He has? Please page him and say he's wanted in X-ray."

"Doctor Potts! Calling Doctor Potts! Doctor Potts to X-ray," O Crispin could hear the public address system repeating in the hall. Within a few minutes, Doctor Potts was in the room, all out of breath.

"Is it bad — that Berry — Berryfield X ray? Is that what you wanted me for, Doctor Waverly?"

The woman in the white coat looked sternly at him.

"Very bad," she said. "Since when, Doctor Potts, have you been using this hospital's facilities for animals?"

"Animals?"

"Chipmunks." She held out the X-ray envelope to him. "Here's a picture — supposed to be Dorothea Berryfield. But it seems Dorothea is really a chipmunk."

O Crispin grew hot to the tips of his ears. Was this Doctor Waverly calling him a chipmunk? "I'll chipmunk her," he thought.

But down below, Doctor Potts was laughing.

"You're joking," he said. "Mrs. Berryfield is no chipmunk. Maybe she's a mouse, but not a chipmunk."

Doctor Waverly was not amused. She looked at Doctor Potts more severely than before. He flinched from her glance, pulled the X ray out of its envelope, and held it to the light. He frowned. He turned the picture on its side, upside down, on the other side, and right side up again, frowning more and more and becoming very red in the face. He looked again at the envelope.

" 'Berryfield, Mrs. Dorothea,' " he muttered. "Nonsense! There's some mistake. Must be!"

"I doubt it," said Doctor Waverly. "In the eight years I've been hospital radiologist, Fred has never marked a picture wrong. Of course he's a bundle of nerves, but careless? Never!" She glanced into the hall. "Here he is now. Fred, we were looking for you. Did you X-ray a chipmunk today? What's up? You're white as a sheet."

The cameraman stood in the doorway and gave a swift glance around the room.

"A chipmunk, no," he said, "but a mouse, yes. At two o'clock. It's filed under 'Berryfield.' Where did the mouse go?"

"Never mind where the mouse went. Who ordered the X ray?"

"He did." Fred looked apologetically at Doctor Potts. "But we do have to find the mouse. It must be still in this room somewhere. Miss Carpenter hates them and says she won't work here until it's gone." Fred was staying near the door as he spoke. "I'm not exactly wild about mice myself. We've been at a standstill for two hours."

Doctor Waverly frowned at Doctor Potts.

"Out there," she said, "are six patients — three of them elderly — waiting for X rays. Your mouse — *your mouse*," she repeated with scornful emphasis, "is keeping them waiting."

"This is ridiculous," thought O Crispin. "I'm not his mouse, or anybody else's mouse. I am my own mouse." He stood up straight and proud, even though the change of position sent horrible twinges through his tail. His electric-blue helmet mirrored one of the bright overhead lights and flashed as his head moved. Fred the cameraman saw it.

"There he is!" he cried. "There he is now! See him! Oh, Lord!" he groaned. "What will he do to that beautiful camera?"

Doctor Waverly spoke sharply.

"Pull yourself together, Fred. Wailing won't help. Besides, someone's coming."

It was the hospital superintendent, followed by a janitor with a ladder, and Nurse Carpenter and Mrs. Berryfield bringing up the rear. The superintendent strutted through the door, as round and fussy as a sparrow.

"All right," he said. "Where is it? We can't have this hospital thrown into an uproar by a little nuisance like a mouse. Fred, Doctor Waverly, Doctor Potts — where is it?"

" 'A little nuisance'! Is that what he calls the Champion of Merrimack County?" snorted O Crispin to himself. He wagged his helmeted head, as if to say to the people below, "here I am. I dare you to come after me!"

The janitor set his tall stepladder close to the X-ray camera.

"That's the idea," said Fred. "If you go up the ladder a step or two, he'll jump down on the table. There's nowhere else he can go."

"Isn't there?" thought O Crispin. "Does that Fred suppose I'm just some ordinary hickory-dickory-dock mouse?"

He kept his beady little eyes on the janitor, who was now

coming up the ladder. He particularly watched the frames of the janitor's glasses and, even more particularly, the screws in the hinges of the frames. As soon as he could see the slots in the screws in the hinges of the frames of the janitor's glasses, he knew it was time to move. He leaped — right into the bristly stubble of the janitor's short-cut hair.

The janitor clung to the ladder with one hand and clutched at his scalp with the other. But O Crispin was already gone, leaping across to the electric cable that hung in thick, snaky loops at the side of the X-ray camera. Up and down and up the cable he ran, and before the janitor could move the ladder to reach him, he had stepped off onto the shiny steel track of the overhead trolley.

By now his tail felt as if it had been knotted around a hot pipe. He wanted to lie down and howl. But he was O Crispin, Champion of Merrimack County, so he couldn't do that. Instead, he clamped his teeth tightly together, letting not even a whimper escape. He crouched low on the track, waiting to see what would happen next.

They tried every kind of trick to dislodge him from his safe perch. When they rolled the camera trolley to and fro on the track, he didn't run away from the wheels; he merely hopped up on the trolley and went for a ride. When Doctor Waverly snapped an elastic band at him, he caught it out

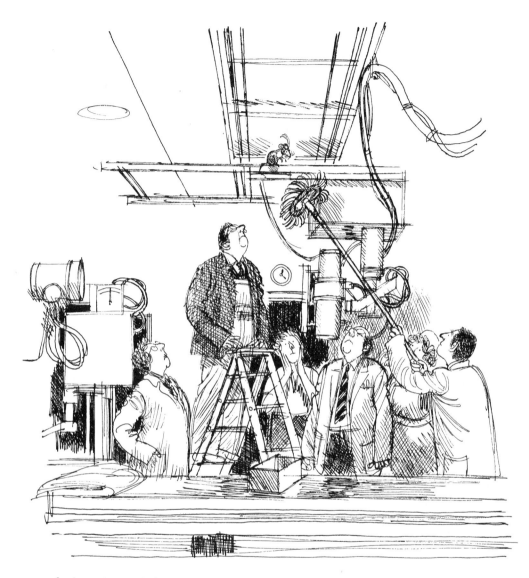

of the air and hung it round his neck for an ornament.

They poked at him with mop handles and said "Boo!" at him from every direction. But nothing they could do either frightened or annoyed him enough to make him leave the track.

"I know!" The superintendent snapped his fingers. "We'll try food!"

He ordered a piece of apple pie with cheese sent up from the kitchen, and presently the hospital dietician herself brought it, hot and steaming under a metal dome. The janitor fetched a long pole with rubber fingers at the end, which he kept just for unscrewing burned-out light bulbs in the high ceiling of the hospital sun-room. He balanced the dish of pie on the fingers. Then very slowly he lifted it until the rim of the plate rested against the track where O Crispin crouched.

The pie smelled heavenly and the cheese looked like the dream of a birthday party. But O Crispin didn't move.

"Do they think," he snorted to himself, "that I am so simple-minded that I can be bamboozled with apple pie in broad daylight?"

After five minutes, they all had stiff necks from watching, and the janitor's arms were tired. He lowered the dish of pie, removed it from the fingers at the end of the pole, sniffed it, and shook his head.

"Stale," he said. "No wonder!"

"Nonsense!" snapped the dietician, replacing the metal

dome on the plate with a clatter. "Our hospital pie is delicious. He's not hungry, that's all."

The superintendent growled that they had trouble enough without arguing over the pie. He turned to Doctor Potts.

"Well, Potts," he said, "I understand that's your patient up there. He'd better be a rich mouse, because somebody's going to pay a whopping big bill for tying up the X-ray room all afternoon. What do you suggest we do next?"

"My patient, maybe," said Doctor Potts, "but Mrs. Berryfield's mouse. What does *she* think?"

"I'm not her mouse, either," muttered O Crispin. "She's *my* Berryfield. But I am glad they're asking her advice. She can be pretty sensible sometimes."

Until now, Mrs. Berryfield had stood in the doorway with Nurse Carpenter, looking on. She had seen how the mouse treated their attempts to get him down and so, when they all turned to her, she was ready with some advice.

"Imagine yourselves in the mouse's place," she said. "He's brave, but he is proud, too. I think we ought to put this shoebox on the X-ray table, with your plate of apple pie inside it. Then we should turn out all the lights and leave the room, and see what happens."

O Crispin smiled. Even if Mrs. Berryfield wasn't a mouse, she certainly knew how to feel like a mouse and think like a mouse. That was what counted. Perhaps her mouth was watering like his at sight of the apple pie!

O Crispin shut his eyes and wished. And wished. And wished. He imagined the taste of the pie, but mostly he imagined his teeth cutting into the piece of cheese he had seen on the pie — a huge and beautiful piece of cheese, bigger than the postage stamps on Mr. Berryfield's desk, and as thick as Mrs. Berryfield's potholder.

After a minute, he opened his eyes and — glory be to Berryfield! — everyone had left the room. There was just time to notice where they had put the plate of pie in the open shoebox, on the X-ray table below him, when out went the light.

9

FOR O CRISPIN, the next hour was a happy dream and a nightmare mixed together.

The climb down from the camera trolley would have been easy enough if his tail didn't hurt. But it did, terribly. He had to stop every few inches to wipe his eyes. They kept filling up with tears, no matter how hard he clenched his jaws or how often he reminded himself that he was the Champion of Merrimack County.

But after that he had his reward.

There were moments of unbelievable rapture, as he lay stretched out on the top crust of the apple pie, with his nose almost touching the cheese, and waited until the pain in his tail had disappeared like the last rumbles of a thunderstorm, while the fragrance of the cheese flooded into his nostrils.

Once he started eating, he went at the chunk of cheese like a shipwrecked sailor — not chisel and chip, but gobble and gulp. He had never had so much food to himself in all his life. What was more, many hours had passed since he had breakfasted on four dry cracker crumbs under the Berryfields' refrigerator.

When Mrs. Berryfield crept into the darkened X-ray room and slid the cover over the shoebox, O Crispin hardly noticed. He just kept eating. He could tell that the box was being carried somewhere, and for a while he was aware of the rumble of a car's engine.

Now and then he heard a murmur of voices outside the box, but he was too busy eating to pay much attention to what they said — even when Doctor Potts told Mrs. Berryfield that the tail was not broken, only dislocated. It could be bandaged with a splint, once it was set.

When the cheese was nearly gone, O Crispin began to feel full and ate more slowly. Mrs. Berryfield was telling the doctor he must arrange the bandage so as not to interfere with riding a bicycle.

"Oh?" the doctor responded. "Then tell me, where does he usually carry his tail when he goes for a ride? In his pocket?"

"No, he had it hooked over one shoulder the only time I've seen him riding. Mice don't have pockets."

"No pockets? What a waste of trousers!"

"But they don't wear trousers, Doctor."

"Perhaps they would, if they understood the importance of pockets. Now, if this fellow had had his tail in a pocket instead of dangling any old way over his shoulder, it might never have been hurt."

In the darkness of the shoebox, O Crispin wondered how his legs would look in trousers. Would they be a handicap in racing?

"Maybe," he said to himself, "Mother could make me a special pair of racing trousers, with a tail-pocket at the back."

At last, nothing was left of the cheese but the smell of it on the pie crust, and O Crispin stopped to look at the pie. A whole wedge! All to himself! It was the chance of a lifetime. Stuffed or starving, a mouse would be crazy not to taste it, at least.

So he took some bites of the crust and, to tell the truth, he was quickly satisfied and felt drowsy. He lay down in a soft fold of Mrs. Berryfield's towel. By the time Doctor Potts cautiously took the lid off the box at his own office, O Crispin was fast asleep, snoring as only a very well fed mouse can snore.

Doctor Potts's gentle hands managed to lift him out of the box, and even to pop the displaced tailbone back in line with the others, without waking him. But it gave him a dreadful dream.

He dreamed he had backed into his grandfather's souvenir mousetrap. His tail was caught and hurting furiously, and his little sister, Q Myrtle, was dancing around, pointing and saying, "Look at O Stupid! Look at O Stupid!" He kicked at the mousetrap with all his might, but could not get free.

Mrs. Berryfield and the doctor noticed that one of his hind legs twitched feebly. That was all they knew about the dream.

"Brave mouse!" murmured Mrs. Berryfield. "Imagine it! Not a squeak!"

"All very well and good," said Doctor Potts, "but they never taught us at medical school how to put a splint on a dislocated tail. Don't expect anything elegant."

O Crispin's nightmare about the mousetrap was followed by solid, dreamless sleep. He awakened to find himself lying on a white table. His sore tail hung from his hips like an anchor. In dismay, he turned to look.

There it was, wrapped round and round in sticking plaster until it was at least as thick and heavy as the nail his family had used to pry Grandfather out of the mousetrap. Doctor Potts had tied a red ribbon around it to make it look like Christmas, but it still felt like a crowbar.

O Crispin's heart sank as he remembered the State Bicycle Rodeo. How could he be ready to race in three days with a handicap like this?

Mrs. Berryfield was worried too. Although she hadn't told Doctor Potts, he saw it in her face.

"It's no good, is it?" he said. "The bandage."

Mrs. Berryfield didn't want to hurt his feelings but she had to consider the mouse too.

"He'll never be able to manage that on a bicycle," she said. "Even if he did have trousers and pockets, what help would they be?"

Doctor Potts scowled at the bandaged tail.

"I suppose you're right," he admitted. "Yes, I'm sure you are. Talk to him, will you, or sing to him, while I get that miserable stickum off and try again."

Mrs. Berryfield sat on a low stool, with her chin on the edge of the table where O Crispin was. He darted a nervous glance at her and crouched very still. By the tickle on his upper lip, he knew his whiskers were trembling.

"It's not because I'm scared of her," he told himself. "They wiggle when I breathe in and out, and I just can't help it."

As Doctor Potts worked on the new bandage, Mrs. Berryfield told stories, the kind of stories she thought, and hoped, this young mouse might enjoy: stories about banquets in

sugar bowls, picnics in potato bins, and bicycle races in bath-tubs.

When her imagination ran dry, she began to sing softly, songs like "Grandfather's Clock," "My Bonnie Lies over the Ocean," "Clementine," and "Daisy, Daisy." She wasn't sure how the mouse would feel about looking "sweet upon the seat of a bicycle built for two," so when she came to that, she simply hummed the tune and pretended to have forgotten the words.

Once she heard the doctor chuckle and asked what was amusing him.

"I never thought," he said, "that I'd see sensible Dorothea Berryfield singing to a mouse!"

"Never mind that," she told him. "Keep working. It must be three or four o'clock already."

"Bless my soul, no!" he said. "Where has the afternoon gone? It's nearly five!"

10

SAM THE SAMPLE HORSE was in no hurry. Whatever Harry and Janet called out to Bangs the Blacksmith, and whatever Bangs said to Sam, the four numbered hooves continued to dawdle along. Scolding, praise, slaps on the rump — nothing helped.

"It's no use," Harry told Janet disgustedly, and loud enough for the horse to hear. "The old nag must have grown up in a family of turtles."

But the procession did finally creep up the last slope to Bel-Air Park and arrive at the Berryfields' house. Janet saw that her mother wasn't back yet, because two deliverymen were standing on the doorstep with packages beside them.

While the blacksmith tied Sam to a sycamore tree, Janet ran up the path.

"Berryfield?" said one of the deliverymen. "We were about ready to quit waiting. Sign here, please." He handed

Janet a yellow receipt and the shortest pencil she had ever tried to hold. "What's up?" he added. "You folks must be infested."

Janet printed her name on the receipt and looked at him, puzzled.

"I was at the phone when your dad called," the delivery-man explained.

" 'Bring all the traps you've got,' he said.

" 'All we've got?' I said. 'Are you sure? That'd be about six dozen.'

" 'Six what?' your dad said. 'We need at least six.'

" 'Then I guess you want 'em all,' I said. It sounds crazy to me, but—" the deliveryman sighed, handing Janet a car-ton, "there they are, all six dozen of 'em."

Janet read the big lettering on the carton and shivered. "Sure-Fire," it said. "72 Traps."

The second deliveryman was growing impatient.

"You'll need this too." He thrust a shopping bag into Janet's hands. "Without this a trap's no good. And seventy-two times no good is still no good."

Janet signed his receipt and looked in the bag. Cheese! A chunk of yellow cheese as big as a grapefruit!

"You people are going to be up half the night setting traps," the first man laughed. "I pity the mice!"

Harry put an arm around Janet's shoulders.

"Come on," he said. "You should see your face. If it gets any longer, Brother Bangs'll mistake you for his horse! Let's go inside. We've got work to do."

It was no simple matter to fasten the mouse's tube and tire to the watch wheel. And time was short.

They wasted precious minutes by letting Silvester Pye work on it because he was used to handling tiny wheels. The trouble was, he had left his little watchmaker's magnifier at his shop and his fingers trembled as he held the wheel at arm's length to see it.

"So much depends on it," the old man explained as he fumbled with the parts. "I keep thinking of all those traps. If we don't get this put together soon — oh dear! Now I've done it! I've dropped the wheel, that's what I've done!"

Down they all went on their knees on the Berryfields' living room carpet to search for the wheel. The carpet was decorated with a spotty pattern of forget-me-nots, and by the time they found the wheel among the forget-me-nots it was a quarter past five.

Everyone agreed that Janet should try next.

"Her eyes are younger than mine," Silvester Pye said, "and her hands won't be so clumsy."

They all encouraged her not to give up, and at last she wheedled and pushed and wished the tube and tire into place in the shallow groove Doctor Norton had made around the wheel. The valve stuck through a neat hole he had drilled for it.

Then the blacksmith braced the bicycle between his thick thumbs while Harry attached the new wheel, tight enough not to wobble and loose enough to spin freely.

"And now," said Silvester Pye, "I suppose you'll be wanting to put some air in that tire."

"Air!" exclaimed Janet. "Of course! But where will we find a tire pump for a mouse's bicycle?"

"Here we go again!" groaned Harry. "Grease my gears with marshmallow, Jan Berryfield, if that mouse of yours isn't almost more trouble than he's worth!"

Janet looked at the bicycle in despair. A tire pump? Could they use the bulb of the horn on the mouse's handlebars? No, it was too big. Maybe the cake decorator in the pantry would do. She dashed off and came back with it in less than a minute.

"Here!" Doctor Norton said. "Let me. I use squirters like this every day in my work." He pressed down the plunger three times sharply. Was air going into the tube? Harry felt of it.

"Whoa!" he cautioned. "One more shot of air and we'd have had a blowout!"

"BONG!"

They all jumped. The clock in the hall was chiming. "BONG, BONG," it continued, as Janet listened and counted. "BONG, BONG, BONG."

"Six o'clock! And I think I hear a car!" Janet glanced wildly around the room. "It's too late to leave. You'll have to hide."

Bangs and Doctor Norton dropped out of sight behind a sofa. Harry disappeared behind the door. Janet was stuffing the bicycle in her pocket, when Silvester Pye popped his white head in from the hall.

"Bless us and save us!" he gasped. "Scared me half out of my wits! That clock of yours—"

"Quick!" said Janet. "Don't talk, Mr. Pye! Whatever you were doing in the hall, come in here and hide yourself! It's six o'clock."

The old watchmaker didn't move.

"But no, Miss Janet. It isn't. Your clock is wrong. That's why I opened it — to see why — why it was running half an hour fast. I—" he covered his ears with his hands, "I didn't expect it would start to strike."

"Then it couldn't have been Daddy's car I heard!" Janet crossed to the window and looked out.

Harry abandoned his hiding-place behind the door, talking as he came.

"For the love of Mike, Uncle! One of these days, you're going to bounce my pendulum right off its hinges! Come now; put your inquisitive hands in your pockets and stay in this room where we can watch you."

In the confusion, no one had heard the front door open and shut. Now, just as the blacksmith and the dentist were getting to their feet behind the sofa on the other side of the room, Mrs. Berryfield appeared in the doorway with the precious shoebox in her hands and Doctor Potts peering over her shoulder.

She stared — at Bangs and Doctor Norton, then at Harry and Silvester Pye, then back again, as if her head was a weather vane that a changeable breeze was blowing to and fro.

Janet ran and hugged her.

"Mom! At last! Is he — is he all right?"

"If you don't knock him out of my hands. But, Janet, who are all these people? Are they waiting to see Daddy? Or what?"

"To see Daddy? Jeepers, no! They've been hiding so they wouldn't. I mean, so *he* wouldn't. But, Mom, can he ride his bike? Mom — are you listening?"

Doctor Potts interrupted.

"I put a bandage on his tail, Janet. It ought to work, though I can't be sure till I see him on his machine. That's what I'm here for."

"But it's late," Janet said. "At least—" she looked at Silvester Pye, "at least, I think so."

Mr. Pye pulled out a fat silver pocket watch, snapped it open, and held it as far from his eyes as he could reach.

"Half past five," he said.

"If it's running," Bangs the Blacksmith rumbled in an undertone.

"And if the works aren't scrambled," Harry added.

Mrs. Berryfield gave them nervous glances.

"Janet, dear, do you know who these men are?"

When Janet had explained, as fast as she could, that they had all helped repair the broken bicycle, Mrs. Berryfield smiled at them weakly.

"Oh, I see," she said. "You all helped. A bicycle repairman — yes, of course. And a watchmaker and a — blacksmith, and a dentist!" She looked at Janet in bewilderment. "And you said they came here with you to hide from Daddy?"

"No indeed, ma'am," Bangs protested. "We are here to see that famous mouse ride his bike. Like the gentleman who came with you." He nodded at Doctor Potts.

"Please, then," said Janet. "Let's get started. There's not even half an hour left!"

11

"LOOK AT HIM!" whispered Mrs. Berryfield. "How he holds his head up! How handsome he is! See that beautiful curly hair on his throat! Look at his tail!"

O Crispin was provoked at being complimented like this, almost to his face. But he was also pleased, very pleased.

"There she goes again," he thought, "talking like my own mother. Still, the way that doctor fixed me, I imagine I do look pretty special!"

He had always envied beavers for their wide, slip-slap tails, shown in pictures in his Social Studies book at school, and wished his own tail were not such a skinny little whip. But now, with his new bandage, he stepped out of the shoebox onto the bathroom floor looking as much like a beaver as a mouse ever could.

Doctor Potts had whittled a pair of thin, flat sticks to the right length, and sandwiched the dislocated tail between them. Then he had put enough tape around the sandwich to hold it all together. The bandaged tail was as wide as its owner and stiff as a canoe paddle.

Although it wasn't so heavy as Doctor Pott's first bandage, it was clumsy and the doctor and Mrs. Berryfield had been worried that one mouse could never drag it along all by himself.

"I know what to do," Doctor Potts had chuckled. "A fisherman like me knows what to do. We'll hang it from a fishing rod."

He slipped the red cockade from its socket on O Crispin's crash helmet, and fitted in its place a flexible wooden stick, thinner than a toothpick and only a little longer than the mouse himself.

"There's his fishing rod," Doctor Potts said. "Now, we'll give him a hook and line."

He tied a nylon thread to the top of the rod and bent a little wire hook to hang on the loose end of the thread. The thread was just long enough so that, when the hook was in position under the bandaged tail, the rod drew back like a spring and held the tail off the ground.

"As if he had a fish on the hook!" exclaimed Mrs. Berryfield.

"Or as if he had flicked the line over his head and hooked the seat of his own pants," laughed Doctor Potts, "the way I did when I was a boy — more than once. I only hope that chin strap is strong enough. If it breaks and his helmet comes off, I hate to think what could happen to his tail!"

As O Crispin stepped out now on the Berryfields' bathroom floor, he remembered that talk about the chin strap. He could feel it tugging his head high. If that was their reason for thinking he looked handsome, they ought to be able to see he couldn't help it. His beaver-tail pulled on the fishing line, the fishing line pulled on the rod, and the pull of the rod was nearly prying off his helmet. And of course the chin strap, which held it all together, pulled up his chin.

"So my tail is hanging from my chin!" he chuckled. "It's crazy, but it works!"

There was a murmur of admiration from everyone, especially the four men who had helped mend O Crispin's bicycle and now saw the mouse himself for the first time.

"I should bow graciously to them," O Crispin thought. "If I can."

He did manage to bend his neck a little and, of course, when his head came down his tail went up, as if one end was saying "thank you," while the other end said "phooey to you!" But O Crispin didn't know that. He was more interested in seeing what had been done to his bicycle.

It stood propped against the pile of paperback books that held up one corner of the tub. O Crispin looked closely at the new front wheel. He squeezed the tire, rolled the machine a short distance without mounting it, lifted the front end off the floor and spun the new wheel with his toe.

"Will he have the nerve to get on, do you think? With that bandage and all?" Mrs. Berryfield whispered to Doctor Potts.

"Sh!" Doctor Potts said. "Wait and see! If I were a mouse, I'd be a timid mouse. You wouldn't catch me on a bicycle at all, even without a bandage. But I can tell you one thing: this mouse has the heart of a lion."

O Crispin's heart gave a great leap in his chest. "Heart of a lion!" Doctor Potts ought to know. Perhaps he had seen it in the X ray. Perhaps he had listened to it with that stethoscope which he always had hanging around his neck.

A mouse with the heart of a lion shouldn't be afraid to ride the mended bike. He shouldn't let a few bandages scare him. If these people saw that a champion with the heart of a lion wasn't brave enough to try it, what would they think of ordinary mice?

He tugged his chin strap into a more comfortable position, swung a leg over the bicycle saddle, and away he went in a wide circle around the bathroom floor. It was a glorious feeling, to be sailing along on his bike again!

"M' gosh, mouse!" cried out Bangs the Blacksmith, flattening himself against the wall. "You trying to take my toes off? Or what?"

The Champion banked sharply, skidding on the smooth linoleum so close to Mrs. Berryfield that she uttered a little shriek of excitement and alarm.

The new front wheel was running well, but this flat bathroom floor didn't really put it to the test. For a proper trial, he would have to get back in the racecourse where he had had the accident.

Besides, there was more to be tested than the wheel and Doctor Pott's fishing pole. O Crispin knew he must find out if he still had the courage of a champion. And didn't he owe it to these people who had helped him, to show them what the Champion of Merrimack County could do?

A wooden towel rack with zigzag scissor legs, standing close to Mr. Berryfield's bathtub, had been O Crispin's ladder to the rim of the tub this morning. He was glad to see it still there. It had been a stiff climb for a mouse pushing a bicycle. Now, with the added weight of his bandage, it would be even harder.

Up the first steep section of the towel rack he toiled. Above, there was another section still to be climbed before he could step across to the tub.

Janet never saw the mouse's struggle on the towel rack leg. She had remembered something more important: the soap in the bottom of the tub — that treacherous sliver of soap. Suppose the mouse ran his bike into it again!

Yes, it was still there. Worse yet was that terrible scratch along the floor of the tub. How could she have forgotten about that?

Leaning over, and holding to the rim of the tub with one hand, Janet could just reach the soap. She raked her fingers against it and it came loose easily.

But now the scratch. It was a brute of a scratch, almost half the length of her father's precious new tub. If he had ordered seventy-two mouse traps when a mouse overturned his can of nails, he would blow the roof off the house when he saw this! There wasn't a chance in the world that he would overlook it. Unless — Janet's imagination began to race — unless she could hide it? Cover it? Paint it white?

She looked desperately around the bathroom for ideas.

Everyone else was too intent on watching the mouse to notice her.

Her eye lit on the family's three toothbrushes hanging in a row beside the sink. Hers had a white patch on the handle. White! Dried toothpaste! Of course! Toothpaste! It might wash off eventually, but at least it would cover the scratch until she and her mother could find a better way to hide it.

Holding the tube down close to the tub, Janet squeezed out a ribbon of white along the scar. She stood up and looked at it with satisfaction: the scratch was invisible. Moreover, the toothpaste had a gloss just like the enamel surface. Now all they had to do was keep Daddy out of the tub and steer him away from looking at it too closely, until — when? How long would it be before dry toothpaste washed off?

Oh no! There was something else! Right this minute, the mouse was climbing the towel rack to go for a ride in the tub. What if he rode into the fresh, slippery toothpaste? How could she warn him?

Janet found the answer to this problem right in her hand: the yellow toothpaste cap. Everyone knew how the street crews kept cars from driving across freshly painted lines in the middle of the road. She could do it too.

She leaned over the tub again and set the yellow cap at one end of the stripe of toothpaste. It looked very much like the yellow wizards' hats used on roads. But there ought to be more than one.

In the cabinet over the bathroom sink, Janet quickly found two more tubes from which she unscrewed the caps: a red one on a tube of liniment, and a blue one on a tube of shaving cream. They didn't match the toothpaste cap, but they would have to do.

Meanwhile, O Crispin was lifting his bicycle across to the bathtub rim. He looked down the long white slope, feeling the old thrill in his veins, and saw the three colored tube-caps showing up brightly on the white enamel. Someone was making sure there would be no accidents today! He remembered how his machine had gone out of control down there, and shivered. Maybe Doctor Potts was right about his heart, but even lions must sometimes be afraid.

Watching him, the people in the bathroom stood motionless. The room was absolutely silent. Suddenly, someone's ankle-joint creaked. O Crispin jumped and jerked around to look, but he turned too fast. The fishing rod swung the opposite way and brought his bandaged tail flying around to the side. If he hadn't swung back again just in time, he would have lost his balance and toppled into the tub.

"Watch it, mouse!" cried Silvester Pye in his reedy voice, "or that double-acting compound pendulum on your hat'll be the death of you!"

But now O Crispin was testing his handbrakes. He clicked the gear control and touched the butt of the fishing rod in the socket on his helmet, to be sure it was firmly set. Everything was ready.

This time down, he would coast. It was important to get the feel of that beaver-tail out behind before he put the bike up to racing speed. He shoved off.

"I don't want to see it!" cried Mrs. Berryfield, covering her eyes. "Tell me when he gets to the bottom."

By the time she said "when," the mouse was already circling under the plug, and by the time Janet told her it was safe to watch, he was headed back on his second run towards the drain.

"Look!" exclaimed Harry. "He's going to give it the gun!"

They all leaned close to the tub. O Crispin stood on the pedals and bore down with his whole weight. The fishing line quivered; the bandaged tail lifted a little in the wind. The bicycle banked sharply and began to climb on the turns.

"Hi, there!"

It was Mr. Berryfield's voice in the hall.

"Hi, there! Janet? Dorothea? Where are you? Who's here?"

12

MR. BERRYFIELD stood at the bathroom door with his hat still on, and stared into the room.

He was not sure just what he expected to see. He had heard strange sounds of running and tumbling break out suddenly in this part of the house when he first called to Mrs. Berryfield and Janet. But everything was quiet now.

Mrs. Berryfield was straightening towels on the rack. Janet had her back against the cellar stairway door, and was busily screwing the cap on a tube of toothpaste. An empty shoebox lay on its side on the floor, with its cover off.

"What in the world is going on here?" Mr. Berryfield demanded. "It sounded like a game of basketball a minute ago. Is somebody sick? Where are the visitors?"

Janet finished capping the toothpaste and put it away.

"Sick? Visitors? Why?" said Mrs. Berryfield, still straightening the towels.

"Well, there's a horse tied to our sycamore tree," Mr. Berryfield said. "And there's a car with doctor's plates on it."

"A horse?" said Janet. "And a car?"

"Tied to our sycamore tree?" said Mrs. Berryfield.

"Yes," Mr. Berryfield replied slowly and patiently, "and he has numbers painted on his hooves."

"On his hooves? Doctor's plates? I never heard of such a thing!" Mrs. Berryfield picked up the shoebox, put the cover on and set the box on the window sill. She began again to fuss with the towel rack. "Do doctors' horses have special numbers?" she asked.

Mr. Berryfield decided it was time to get this conversation under control.

"Dorothea! Are you sure you are all right? You've arranged those towels once already. Now listen to me carefully." He was keeping his voice down, but it had a hard edge as he went on. "There is a horse with numbers on his hooves, and a car with doctor's plates. Also a red and black bicycle built for two. All in front of our house. Did they arrive by themselves? Somebody must be here besides you and Janet."

"A bicycle built for two!" exclaimed Janet. "In front of our house? How exciting!"

Mr. Berryfield threw up his hands.

"I never saw such a family!" he said. "Nobody answers my

questions. You just ask them back at me. Dorothea, if you came home and found a strange bicycle and a doctor's car parked outside, and a — an abandoned horse trampling the grass under our sycamore tree, wouldn't you want to know why?" A thought struck him.

"Oh!" he smiled. "A surprise! Is that it? Is that why you won't answer my questions? I'll bet it's something to do with the tub!"

He went over to the bathtub, crouched and examined the legs.

"H'm," he said. "Still has the paperbacks under this corner. So that's not it. And it's not a soap dish." He stood up and was glancing inside, when a little gasp from Janet made him turn to her.

"Daddy," she said quickly, "out in the kitchen there are some things for you from the hardware store." She took him by the elbow and tugged him away from the bathtub, but he went only a step or two, then pulled loose from her insistent hand.

"Hardware store?" he said. "Oh yes, the traps. And there's cheese, too, isn't there? I'll attend to that after supper. Right now—" he turned back and patted the bathtub, "if I can get a few reasonable questions answered first, I'm looking forward to a good soak in this genuine antique here."

Janet gulped. The toothpaste couldn't possibly be hard enough yet to last through one of Daddy's baths. How could she stop him?

"No, Daddy! Wait!" she pleaded. "First, there's something I've got to talk to you about; a question I've got to ask you. Couldn't you put off your tub till after supper?"

"Will your question take that long? What did you want to ask?"

"Just — if you couldn't wait till after supper."

Mr. Berryfield took off his hat and ran a hand through his thin black hair.

"Did you hear that, Dorothea? First, Jan asks me if I'll put off my soak so she can ask a question; then she says that *is* the question! Something queer is going on here, and I want to know what it is."

Mrs. Berryfield took her husband's arm.

"Don't upset yourself, Arthur," she said. "Janet only meant there's not much time before supper. You know you hate to be rushed when you're having a real soakeroo in the tub! Why not come along out to the living room and put your feet up and read a chapter or two of that new mystery story, and—"

"Wait a minute," Mr. Berryfield protested. "Are you and Jan trying to get me out of this room? Is there something

I'm not supposed to see? Are you telling me I can't have a bath in my own tub when I want to? Such as right now?"

Mrs. Berryfield glanced at Janet. What could they say?

"I've been planning on it all day," Mr. Berryfield went on in a dreamy singsong, beaming down at the bathtub. "I've been thinking about this sensible plug that really plugs the hole; I've imagined myself turning these faucets that are hitched to real pipes. Look at them! Not like those new-fangled ones we used to have that disappeared into the wall where they might leak or break or go on the blink, and nobody know it for a week. But these! Out in the open; nothing secret about them! Hot, Cold; On, Off. This is what I call proper plumbing!"

There was no arguing with that look in his eyes. In a few minutes, Janet felt sure, he would find the scratch in the tub and discover everything else. As he put the plug into the drain hole, she held her breath.

He straightened up, saying nothing, turned on the water, and stood watching as it danced from the spout.

"Beautiful!" he murmured. "See how it puddles and splashes over the—" His words stopped. His smile faded. Janet thought her heart, too, had stopped beating. Mr. Berryfield shut off the water and stared at the drain plug. Then he bent over and felt the bottom of the tub.

"It couldn't be," he said.

"What is it, dear?" said Mrs. Berryfield. "Something wrong?"

"Wrong, yes. The enamel seems to be worn away here, under the faucet. But it can't be. It was all right this morning. I don't understand it."

He pulled the plug. As the last of the water ran out, he got down on his knees beside the tub and again felt with his fingers near the drain.

"Look at this!" He held up fingertips that were white as if he had touched wet paint. He sniffed them. "I know that smell. It's not paint. Come now, Dorothea, Janet, do you know anything about this? What is it?"

"Soap?" suggested Mrs. Berryfield timidly.

"Marshmallow?" said Janet.

He sniffed his fingers again and touched the tip of his tongue to one of them.

"No," he said. "Not soap. And it's too pepperminty for marshmallow. Might be toothpaste. But what's it doing in the tub?" He looked sharply at Janet. Janet looked at her mother for help, and Mr. Berryfield saw their eyes meet. "Oh!" he said. "So this *is* part of the big mystery! Let's see what else I can find out."

He took a sponge from the edge of the sink, ran water on it, and began vigorously wiping out the bottom of the tub. After a few sweeps of his arm, he sat back on his heels, staring at the sponge. It was white. His arm slumped on the edge of the tub. He spoke in a low voice, angry or miserable, or both, without turning his head.

"How did it happen?"

Janet and Mrs. Berryfield came forward and looked over his shoulders. The sponge had cleared away all the toothpaste, and the scratch now showed up, dark and ugly, for its full length.

"How did it happen?" Mr. Berryfield said again. "I want to know how it happened. After all the trouble I had getting this tub — to find it ruined so soon!"

No one said a word. Mr. Berryfield waited for Janet or her mother to speak, but they could think of nothing to say. And at just that moment all three of them heard a sudden faint thump in the enclosed attic stairway.

"What was that?" said Mr. Berryfield. "Something's on the stairs."

"On the stairs? Mice, I imagine." Mrs. Berryfield stationed herself against the stairway door and faced her husband.

"Nonsense!" he snapped. "Mice don't thump. That was a thump and you know it was. You jumped like a rabbit. Why not look and see?"

"The door's locked," she said, rattling the handle with one hand behind her. "How could anything be there?"

"If you won't look, I will," he said. "Maybe nothing's there, but we all heard it. I don't want to have 'nothing' go bump on those stairs while I'm snoozing in the tub."

He strode across the room and reached behind his wife

for the attic door handle. As she had said, the door seemed to be locked. He motioned her aside, turned the key with one hand, and with the other suddenly pulled the door wide open.

Luckily for him, he stepped back at the same time, for the five men who had been hiding on the attic stairs tumbled out like water through a broken dam and landed in a tangle of arms and legs on the bathroom floor.

13

THE CRASH IN THE BATHROOM shook the cellar stairs enough to make O Crispin's teeth chatter.

Janet had hurriedly hidden him behind the closed cellar stairway door, and he had been crouching there on the top step all this time, listening to the voices in the bathroom. Now he realized that Mr. Berryfield had opened the attic door and might decide to open this one next.

"No more practice today," he said to himself. "I'd better start looking for a safer place to hide."

There was only one path to and from the cellar for a mouse with a bicycle, and that was by a long board Mr. Berryfield had left lying at the side of the stairs. In the dim light, it looked steeper to O Crispin than it had seemed when he came up this morning. But it was really a gentler slope than the end of the tub and, by using his brakes, he coasted to the bottom under good control.

He stopped there and listened. The voices in the bathroom went on talking, and the stairway door stayed shut. So far, so good.

Any ordinary mouse would have known a great deal more than O Crispin did about the Berryfields' new cellar. The rest of his family had explored every inch of it, from the time its cement block walls were built. They had talked about it at meals, and about the three secret ways to get in and out, two leading up through the bathroom walls to the attic, and the other one going outdoors to the garden. Lately, too, the family had laughed about a homemade trap which some of them had explored and robbed of its bait.

But practicing for the big race kept O Crispin too busy to be bothered with things like that. He had never inspected the additions to the house, and when his brothers and sisters were giggling about Mr. Berryfield's mousetrap he had been daydreaming of new and more exciting racecourses.

O Crispin's mother often worried about him.

"If only he had paid attention to his mousecraft lessons while he was going to school," she said, "I would feel better. But it's bicycles, bicycles all the time. He doesn't seem to understand how people feel about us, and what they can do to us." O Crispin had overheard her saying to his father, only yesterday, "I'm just not sure Crispin would know a mousetrap if he saw one."

"Let the boy alone," his father had replied. "I wish I'd had a chance to race bicycles when I was his age. He'll be all right; he'll make a great name for himself yet."

O Crispin had been through the cellar many times, but had never stopped to look around. Enough light came through a small window to show him stacks of short boards leaning against the walls, and Mr. Berryfield's workbench in the middle of the room, with an unswept litter of wood shavings on the floor around it. Where could he hide?

Pushing his bicycle, O Crispin threaded his way among the shavings. One of his wheels jarred the bottom of a big shaving that curled high up like a breaking wave, and it toppled over, scattering sawdust on him as it fell. He sneezed explosively.

To him the sneeze sounded as loud as a window breaking. Surely they would hear it upstairs and come after him! He stood rock-still, listening. No, it seemed they hadn't noticed. Maybe you had to be a mouse to hear a sneeze like that!

He kept on until he arrived under the workbench, where the floor should have been clearer. But it wasn't. That very morning, in furious disgust, Mr. Berryfield had pushed his unsuccessful mousetrap in there, out of sight, before leaving for work.

O Crispin gazed up at the trap curiously. He had no idea what it might be. It seemed to be a box, made of wood, somewhat larger than Mrs. Berryfield's shoebox. On the end nearest him, close to the floor, there was a round hole big enough to walk through. O Crispin inspected all four sides of the box, and when he had returned to where he began, without finding any other opening, he knew that this hole must be the only entrance.

What was inside? He crept close to the hole and sniffed.

His pointed nose quivered as it picked up several smells mixed together, and began to give them names. There was the sharp turpentiney smell of new pine wood; the smell of Mr. Berryfield's hands; a distinct mouse smell, which probably meant that some of O Crispin's family had been inside; and then, confused with those other smells, a gone-away cheese smell. That was worth investigating. Perhaps it didn't make a mouse's tongue tingle as a real there-it-is cheese smell would, but it was double-much better than a never-was cheese smell.

Glancing over his shoulder through the tangle of shavings towards the cellar stairs, O Crispin knew that at any moment Mr. Berryfield might come banging down from the bathroom. And here was a ready-made hiding place, with a door big enough for a mouse and much too small for Mr. Berryfield. And with a gone-away cheese smell inside!

Whiskers alert, he put his head in the hole. Bang! The rod on his crash helmet ran into the side of the box. He had forgotten all about that.

There was nothing to do but loosen his chin strap and let the helmet slip back on his head. He winced as his beaver-tail came down slap on the floor, but the rod — now lying flat along his back — no longer interfered with entering the box. Again he put his head in the hole.

Needling the darkness inside, his little black eyes made out the beginning of a gentle uphill path, enclosed right and left and above by a mesh of screen wire. Why wait?

It was a tight squeeze to pull the bicycle through the hole beside him. Then up the center of the path he wheeled it, guiding himself by whisker-touch. His dragging tail hurt, so he straightened his helmet again to lift it, and kept on, as the path climbed slowly into the darkness.

The gone-away cheese smell was stronger here. Delicious! O Crispin's eyes, growing big in the dark, stared ahead and saw that the path he was on ended at a step, which leveled out to make a sort of shelf. His nose told him the cheese had been on the shelf. As far as he could see, it was all gone. Why not stand on his hind legs against the steps and make sure?

He reached for the cheese shelf, but as he did so it seemed to become higher — and higher.

URK! What was happening?

The path he stood on was going down, dropping away under his feet like an elevator.

Wildly, he looked back and saw the doorway hole disappearing. The bottom end of the sloping path was rising in the air. The path was like a seesaw! A giant seesaw! O Crispin's eyes and stomach told him that his end was going down.

Down it went, faster and faster, until it stopped with a THUMP, and he and his bicycle rolled off the end of the path.

He scrambled quickly to his feet, and saw the end of the see-saw from which he had just fallen going up in the air again. He grabbed at it and missed. In a moment, it stopped with a click, like a lock fastening, high up and hopelessly out of reach.

"Well," he said to himself, "that's the most complicated, inconvenient way I ever saw of getting into a box. But what a wonderful place this will be to hide until the coast is clear!"

He examined the inside of the box and found it was lined with strong wire mesh on all sides, top and bottom. There was certainly no other opening. None at all.

"Beautiful!" he thought. "No one bigger than me can get in. But — when the alarm is over, how will I get out?"

The downhill end of the seesaw path was firmly wedged at the entrance hole, as it had been in the beginning, absolutely blocking that exit. Floor, walls, and ceiling were solid and covered with wire.

"A fine champion I am," he muttered. "This perfectly safe hiding place is no better than a prison. I wouldn't be surprised if it's some kind of a trap. In fact, I'll bet that's just what it is. Perfectly safe! Wow!"

14

WHILE O CRISPIN was getting caught in the home-made trap, the five men who had spilled out of the attic stairs were untangling themselves in the bathroom above. Mr. Berry-field watched in silence and waited to hear how they would explain themselves.

"Whew!" sighed Bangs the Blacksmith, dusting himself off. "It's good to move around again!"

Silvester Pye tried to stand up, then collapsed on the floor and rubbed his ankle.

"My foot's asleep," he said with a little grin. "That's why I lost my balance."

Doctor Potts straightened his necktie, stuffed the loose end of his stethoscope into his breast pocket, and turned to Mr. Berryfield.

"If you are wondering about us, Arthur," he said, "we can explain."

It was a relief to Mr. Berryfield to see one face he knew.

"Doctor Potts! Then the car out there is yours! Is someone here sick? My own wife and daughter won't tell me; perhaps you will. And while you're at it — how did this scratch, this scar, this infernal gouge come in the bottom of my bathtub?"

"A gouge in the enamel?" interrupted Doctor Norton the dentist. He scrambled to his feet, adjusted his pale blue jacket, and peered intently into the tub. "Tut, tut! Look at that! Between you and me, Mr. Berryfield, enamel is my specialty. Did you know, it is one of the hardest of natural substances? No doubt, bathtub enamel is different from dental enamel and it is — as we can all see — more easily scratched. Nevertheless—"

"Very interesting, Doctor!" broke in Harry. "But you're sucking air. The man's not asking for a lecture on the wonders of dental enamel."

Mr. Berryfield smiled gratefully.

"Thank you, Mr. — er—?"

"Harry. Jack-of-all-bicycles."

"Thank you, Harry — Jack," said Mr. Berryfield. "The bicycle out there — is it yours?"

"Feed me a flannel sandwich if it's not my very own," said Harry.

Mr. Berryfield blinked.

"And the horse tied to our sycamore tree?" he asked. "Does he belong to one of these other gentlemen?"

"Sam's mine. He's my sample horse," Bangs explained.

Mr. Berryfield shuddered and shut his eyes. When he opened them again, he looked at Mrs. Berryfield and Janet.

"Who needs a sample? Is he persuading you to buy a horse?"

Janet laughed.

"Don't worry, Daddy. It's a sample horse because it wears four different kinds of shoes."

Mr. Berryfield sat down on the edge of the bathtub and shook his head slowly from side to side.

"I came home," he said, "hoping to have a good hot bath before supper. Instead, I find my tub ruined, strangers falling out of the attic, and my family starting a shoe store for horses. Can't someone tell me, in a few simple words, what all these people are doing here, with their horses and bicycles and flannel sandwiches?"

How could they stop him asking questions, without giving away the whole story of the bicycle mouse? Janet had a wild idea.

"You nearly guessed it before, Daddy. It's part of a big surprise for you."

"I've had enough surprising for one day," growled Mr.

Berryfield. "What I want is a good bath, then some supper, and then to put mousetraps upstairs and down. If there are any more surprises hiding behind the doors of this house, I want to hear about them now."

Silvester Pye looked nervously at his watch.

"Well," he said, "I'd better be going."

Bangs the Blacksmith and Doctor Norton edged towards the door.

"Me, too," said Bangs.

"And I likewise," agreed the dentist.

"Yes," said Doctor Potts. "I can't be of any further help here today."

"Help?" Mr. Berryfield pounced on the word. "Then someone *is* sick? Hold on there!" He reached the bathroom door before the others, and stood there, red-faced and determined.

"The guessing game is over," he said. "I give up. You can spring your surprise now. Nobody leaves this room until I find out who is sick, how my tub got scratched, and what the rest of this — this congregation is doing here."

Mrs. Berryfield took the lapels of his jacket in her hands.

"Arthur," she said. "You mustn't be angry."

"Angry? I'm not angry. Why mustn't I be angry?"

"Because if you're angry, it won't be . . . safe to tell you all you want to know."

Mr. Berryfield let out a long sigh.

"All right," he said. "I'm not angry."

"And you won't be, if we tell you?"

"No, I won't be."

"Promise?"

"I promise."

"Not even if — not even if—"

"For heaven's sake, Dorothea! Even if what?"

Janet thought she'd better help.

"Daddy," she said, "do you promise not to punish anybody, or any—" She broke off.

"Anybody or any what? What else is there to punish?"

"Some people punish horses," Bangs suggested.

"Or dogs," said Janet. "Things like that. Promise?"

"All right. I promise not to punish anybody or any — pet," agreed Mr. Berryfield reluctantly. "Now answer my questions: how did my tub get scratched? Who's been sick? And why are all these strangers here?"

The time had come! The quicker he was told, the better. Janet took a deep breath.

"To see a mouse ride a bicycle. Doctor Potts fixed his broken tail."

"Dislocated," murmured Doctor Potts.

"What?" said Janet.

"Dislocated," Doctor Potts repeated. "It isn't broken."

"Oh, good!" said Janet. "Wait, Daddy! I'm not finished. Mr. Pye found a new front wheel for the bicycle; Doctor Norton whizzed the bumps off the wheel; Harry was the one who knew about Mr. Pye; and who else is there? Oh yes, Mr. Bangs the Blacksmith — he and Sam led us to Doctor Norton. Is that everybody?"

"Stop!" protested Mr. Berryfield. "Back up! Why did you say they came to our house? Something about mice?"

"That's right. None of them ever saw a mouse ride a bike before."

"Neither have I," said Mr. Berryfield, "thank the Lord! They get around fast enough without bicycles. But why would anyone expect to see such a crazy thing here?"

"Mom and I told them they could."

Mr. Berryfield gave his wife a look loaded with reproach.

"Games are games, Dorothea," he said, "but is it fair to Jan to encourage nonsense like that? Bringing every Tom, Dick, and Harry-Jack-of-all-bicycles into our house to — to see a mouse ride a bicycle?" He snorted. "Did you and Jan make up all this folderol so you wouldn't have to tell me how my tub got scratched?"

"Oh no, Arthur!" said Mrs. Berryfield. "We *are* telling you. That's exactly how it happened."

Mr. Berryfield frowned.

"Go on," he said.

"The bicycle skidded — on your soap — and fell over, and scratched the tub as it slid along. And the mouse broke his tail."

"Dislocated," said Doctor Potts.

Mr. Berryfield went to the tub, and stood looking down into it.

"It's a big tub," he agreed, "but anybody can see there isn't room."

"Don't you understand, Daddy?" Janet was becoming exasperated with him. "It was a *mouse's* bicycle."

"A mouse's bicycle? You expect me to believe that? A mouse riding a bicycle in this house? All right. Maybe that much is true. But why in my bathtub?"

"Don't you see? It's perfect! With the ends banked the way they are, it makes a wonderful racecourse!"

"MY TUB?" roared Mr. Berryfield. "A RACECOURSE? For a MOUSE?" Then he relaxed and grinned at her. "What a joker you are, Jan! You almost had me believing it!"

Mrs. Berryfield spoke quietly.

"It's true, Arthur. Janet isn't making it up. We've all seen it. It's true."

Mr. Berryfield scowled at the scratched tub, and at his wife and daughter. They said nothing, and for a few moments neither did he. Then he made up his mind.

"All right," he said. "Where are those traps?"

15

JANET GRABBED at her father's sleeve, but he brushed past her and out the bathroom door, heading for the kitchen.

"No, Daddy!" she pleaded. "You promised!"

If he heard her, he paid no attention. In a moment, he was ripping open the carton of traps.

"Mice!" he exploded. "Mice! Ridiculous! In my beautiful bathtub! On bicycles! It couldn't be! I'll put a stop to that kind of nonsense!"

"But you said if we told you," Janet insisted, "you wouldn't punish anybody or anything."

Mrs. Berryfield had caught up with them.

"Janet's right, Arthur," she agreed. "You did say so."

"Anybody or any *pets* was what I said." Mr. Berryfield peered into the refrigerator. "Where's that cheese? Mice are not pets. Not when my wife and daughter imagine mice are riding bicycles in the bathtub. They're a menace, that's what they are. They're driving you crazy. I'll probably be next."

He found the lump of cheese and began to cut little chunks off it with a paring knife.

"Not this mouse, Daddy," said Janet. "This mouse really is a pet."

"A pet, is he? And he's the one that gouged my bathtub with a bicycle? Maybe now you know why I don't like pets!" Mr. Berryfield jabbed at the cheese, forgetting his other hand that held it steady. "Bam-blazes! Now I've cut my thumb!"

While Mrs. Berryfield bandaged his thumb, she told him he must stand still and listen, because if he began arguing again he'd wave his arms and spoil the bandage.

"Of course pets misbehave sometimes, Arthur," she said. "So do children," said Janet.

"But you give them another chance," Mrs. Berryfield went on. "And people make mistakes too — like cutting their fingers with knives." She pressed down the end of the adhesive tape.

"Ouch!" said Mr. Berryfield. "Can I talk again? If this mouse of yours is a pet, I suppose he comes when you call, does he? And wears a collar? And you feed him? He wags his tail at you, or purrs? Things like that?" Mr. Berryfield began baiting a trap.

"Wait a minute, Arthur. Being a pet doesn't always mean being tame. It can mean being looked after and cared for. Don't forget, I took this mouse to my own doctor when his tail got broken."

"Dislocated." Doctor Potts spoke up from the kitchen door, where he and the others had gathered to watch.

"Mom's right," Janet said. "Being a pet isn't something you do, or whether you wear a collar, or anything like that. It's how people feel about you; if they feed you; if they care when you get hurt; if they don't want you to be caught—" Janet swallowed and looked away, "in a trap."

Mr. Berryfield heard scarcely a word of what they said. By now he had baited four of the hardware store traps and was on his way back to the bathroom. Janet squeezed past him in the hall, ran ahead, and stood against the cellar stairway door.

"No, no, no!" she said. "You promised you wouldn't hurt our mouse. He's our pet, Mom's and mine. If you'd been here this morning, if you'd seen him tearing around in the tub, you'd agree with us. He's probably the only mouse in the world who can do what he can."

Mr. Berryfield laughed grimly.

"I hope he is! And when I get through, there won't be even one. If I ever imagine anything like that, do you know what I'll do? First I'll yell loud enough to scare the critter out of Bel-Air Park for good, and then I'll turn on the cold water and hold my head under it till I wake up! Come, Jan! Your pet is down there, is he? Remember, he's not the only one I'm after. Let me by! I want to set these traps before supper."

But Janet kept her back against the door, and no matter what her father said, she wouldn't move. It had only been an hour since he came home and, for all she knew, the mouse might still be where she had hidden him, on the other side of the door.

Mr. Berryfield was thinking he would have to push her out of the way, but he noticed that all the others had returned to the bathroom and were watching him silently.

"Why are you frowning at me like that?" he growled. "Don't I have a right to do away with the mice in my own house?"

"Of course," said Harry. "Every pesky one of them, except—"

"Except?"

"Except the bike-rider."

"The bathtub-wrecker, you mean."

"Same thing. The pet you promised not to punish."

The doorbell jangled in the hall and Mrs. Berryfield went to answer it.

Mr. Berryfield tried to be patient with Janet.

"Look," he said, "it won't help your so-called pet, to put no traps in the cellar. Mice move around in a house. If there are traps anywhere, any mouse may be caught in them. The only way to save that pet of yours is to find him and tell him from me to stay away from the traps; or else put him in a box."

"But we can't do that. We don't even know where he is — exactly."

"Whistle! Call him! You have ten minutes, starting now."

It seemed only a moment since Mrs. Berryfield had gone to answer the doorbell, but now she was back again, pale and flustered. She slammed the bathroom door behind her.

"They're loose!" she gasped. "Arthur, that was the man from the pet shop."

Mr. Berryfield looked blank.

"The pet shop? What man?"

"He said you had rented eight cats for the night."

"Oh yes! Of course! The pet shop cats!"

"And, Arthur, he opened the top of the basket to show me" — Mrs. Berryfield was almost in tears — "and somehow it came completely off, and now those cats, all eight of them, are loose in the house."

16

"THIS," SAID HARRY, "is an honest-to-gosh, old-fashioned, bang-the-dishpan emergency. Those pet shop cats have been in the mouse-cleaning business for years, and they are real tigers, believe you me! My old Aunt Alice used them once. Real tigers!"

"Tigers!" Mrs. Berryfield leaned against the door. "I'd rather put up with the mice!"

"Maybe you would, Dorothea," said Mr. Berryfield. "But now we've got them both. By morning, it will be good-bye mice. I hope. The pet shop guarantees it."

Bangs the Blacksmith chuckled.

"I'm just wondering," he said, "what those cats'll think when they see our mouse on his bicycle!"

"He'll give them the howling yowlies," said Harry.

"You know," suggested Silvester Pye, "he may be too fast for them."

"And get away!" said Janet.

"Any sensible mouse," Mrs. Berryfield declared, "would just stay in his hole until the cats were gone."

But although Mrs. Berryfield always tried to be sensible, she was not a mouse. She didn't know the stories that were told in O Crispin's family about the pet shop cats. It was one of them that had appeared in Grandfather G Rufus's dream and given him such a scare that he backed into the trap.

They were merciless brutes. They prowled in dark corners with their hard noses close to the floor like bulldozers. It was said that they could light up the inside of a mouse hole by glaring in through the door, and mice had been known to die of terror at the sight of a pet shop cat's eye looking in.

The very idea of being in the same house with them was enough to set any mouse's knees to shaking.

"It's best to take no chances with those butchers," the children were told. "You don't fool crafty, experienced cats like them with old tricks like mouse holes that have back doors."

Forty-three members of O Crispin's family, as well as about a hundred and sixty other mice who weren't his relatives at all, and not counting those that had to be carried because they were too young to run, streamed out of the Berryfields' cellar that night into the daffodil and tulip beds which separated the houses in Bel-Air Park. Going tiptoe and single file by one of the secret ways, they were gone before the cats had half begun to hunt for them.

Only two mice stayed behind. One was O Crispin's cocksure cousin, Fritz. He had laughed at the talk of danger. Even when they began to leave without him, he wouldn't change his mind.

"You're just a lot of fraidy bugs," he told his brothers and sisters. "I don't believe this house is half as dangerous as they say. If it is, I want to find out for myself."

And he did. He had a fine evening, scampering in the abandoned walls and playing with the toys his family had left behind. At about eleven o'clock, he spied a nice piece of cheese just outside one of the mouse holes.

"Look what the rest of them missed!" he laughed as he reached for it.

SNAP!

The other mouse who stayed was O Crispin, still securely boxed in the seesaw trap. Though the cats had soon found him, it did them no good. They could hear, through the trap walls, the faint buzz of his whiskers as he breathed in and out. But the little door was much too small for them to enter.

When they tried to upset the trap and make him fall out,

it wouldn't budge — not even with four of them on their hind legs pushing against it all together. Finally, the lop-eared black tom who was their leader left two guards to pounce on O Crispin if he tried to escape.

O Crispin had felt the hair on his neck uncurl and stiffen until it stood straight out. A voice inside him said, "Stay where you are, mouse! Stay where you are!" But he couldn't have put his head out the door if he had wanted to. The wire screening on the seesaw path kept him from getting anywhere near it.

It was a quiet, unhappy evening for the Berryfield family. Doctor Potts and the others had left after the arrival of the pet shop cats, and the family had eaten supper in silence. Then Mr. Berryfield set a dozen of the new traps in dark corners and ran himself a deep hot bath.

"Why the traps?" Mrs. Berryfield wanted to know. "Don't you trust your tigers?"

"Nonsense!" said Mr. Berryfield. "They aren't tigers — just cats. I know the pet shop guaranteed they would do the job, but I don't like to take chances. It's better to kill each mouse twice than not at all. A few traps will be all to the good."

Janet had finally allowed her father to open the cellar door, so the cats could come and go. She had had to agree with him that the door couldn't be kept shut forever. If the bicycle mouse wasn't safely hidden by now, no one could protect him.

What a relief it had been to find that he was gone from the top step! But where was he? How would he hide his bicycle and himself — especially with that awkward fishing rod in his hat? Were ordinary mouse holes wide enough, or high enough?

Mrs. Berryfield tried to comfort her. After all, she said, this mouse must have been going in and out of mouse holes with his bicycle before today. The only difference now was the bandaged tail and the rod and line.

"Any mouse as clever as ours," Mrs. Berryfield assured her, "could manage it, even if he had a flagpole on his head!" But they both worried, just the same.

Late in the evening, after Janet had gone to bed, Mrs. Berryfield took sudden fright at the snap of the trap that caught foolish Fritz. When she saw the dead mouse, she knew it couldn't be the bicycle mouse, because there was no bandage on his tail. But, until she finally fell asleep, she jumped at every little sound and imagined dreadful things.

Next morning at daybreak, the eight cats held a meeting in front of the seesaw trap. Except for Fritz, not a mouse had they seen all night: nothing but a few disappearing tails. They were angry and hungry.

One of them, a tabby with long front legs, tried reaching into O Crispin's prison through its narrow door, hoping to scoop him out, but all she got for her trouble was a cramp in the shoulder.

Mrs. Berryfield set a pan of milk on the back step for the disappointed cats and there they waited, slurping the milk and grouching about their bad luck, until the pet shop wagon came for them.

"My husband said he has no complaints," Mrs. Berryfield told the driver. "Maybe your cats didn't catch any mice, but he's sure the mice are all gone. He set twelve traps, too, and only one was touched. And that one caught a mouse. He's so sure about it that he packed up the traps and put them away before leaving for work this morning."

That evening, Mrs. Berryfield used the leftover cheese in a big batch of Welsh Rabbit for supper. As Mr. Berryfield lay in his tub, he sang to himself, "This is the life for me!"

Nowhere in the house could he hear the least sound of scratching or nibbling. There were only two things now to spoil his perfect happiness: the gouge in the bottom of the tub, which he feared would soon begin to rust, and the failure of his seesaw trap.

But tomorrow was Saturday. Tomorrow he intended to get rid of that crazy trap. He had no wish to keep it to remind him that it hadn't worked, that he had invented a trap which mice could rob so easily. They had made a fool of him. The trap had made him look like an idiot.

If Dorothea or Janet found out he was planning to destroy it, they would think he had given up. They would think he was admitting that mice were cleverer than he.

Of course that wasn't true. There was just something wrong with the stupid trap. He would get up early tomorrow, before Dorothea or Janet were awake, and deal with it. He would chop it up for kindling wood.

17

JANET KNEW that on Saturday mornings her parents usually slept late. Often she did too, but this Saturday she was roused early by a dream.

In her dream, the mouse was safe. He was back in the bathtub and had what looked like a pair of wings. When he raced down the slope, he actually took off and glided on the wings — bike and all — the whole way to the hanging plug, before settling down!

The dream seemed real enough to be true. Could it be? Janet swung her legs over the side of the bed and put her feet down on the floor as softly as a falling handkerchief. She tiptoed out of her room. If the dream were true, she wanted her father to sleep as long as possible.

But when she arrived in the bathroom, she found the tub empty. It looked exactly as it had yesterday. There was no sign that the mouse had been there in the night.

One thing, however, surprised her. The door to the cellar stairs stood wide open and the light shining out into the room showed that the stairway switch was on.

Softly, Janet crossed the bathroom. Was that a voice, speaking quietly down in the cellar? She leaned her head close to the doorway and listened. Yes, it was a voice, and it sounded like her father's.

How could it be? Why was he up so early? If Mr. Berryfield really was in the shop, who was he talking to? Very cautiously, Janet looked around the side of the opening.

It *was* her father! No doubt at all! He was standing under the hanging light, at his workbench. His back was towards the stairs and it seemed he had not heard Janet's soft footsteps. His homemade trap was on the bench. He had taken off the cover and was holding it in one hand. As Janet watched, he bent over the trap, looked in, and began talking again.

"So it does work, after all! And I have you to thank for showing me! The good-for-nothing mousetrap finally catches one mouse! When I bait it with cheese, I lose the cheese; when I bait it with nothing — I catch you! You must be the stupidest mouse in the world. And I'm the stupidest inventor! A fine pair we are! We come off the same shelf!"

He set down the cover on the end of his workbench, rested both hands, and bent more closely over the open trap.

"With a bicycle, too," he murmured. "Just as they told me! I suppose that's what tipped the seesaw. But what's that funny rig on your head? Are you some kind of an FBI mouse, with a radio in your hat?"

Janet could have let out a yell of joy. The bicycle-mouse — her mouse — was in that box! He must have hidden in it when the cats were hunting and the snap-traps were set. He was alive! But now Daddy had caught him.

Mr. Berryfield was speaking again.

"So the only mouse left is the one that ruined my tub! Saved by my own trap! What should I do with you? You look pretty lively, little fellow, with that perky blue helmet and all, to have been in there since Thursday night without a speck of food." Mr. Berryfield replaced the lid on the trap and rested a hand on it. "I suppose I should have looked yesterday. But how could I know we had a mouse that would walk into a baitless trap? Now what do I do?"

His fingers drummed on the lid.

"Hey, there!" he said suddenly, taking his hand off the trap. "I mustn't do that! It probably sounds like thunder, inside. That's no way for a dimwit inventor to treat his bubble-headed guest. It's not every day one gets a visit from the stupidest mouse in Merrimack County!" He gazed thoughtfully at the trap.

"Thank the Lord I got up early! I thought I had a good reason for coming down to smash this stupid invention when Dorothea and Janet weren't around. Now I've got a much better one. If they knew I'd found their mouse alive and safe in this house, I'd really be in trouble. They were already calling him a pet." He paused. "Confound it! I'm beginning to see why."

"Ar-thur!" It was Mrs. Berryfield calling from the other end of the house.

Janet didn't want to be caught listening at the top of the cellar stairs. She padded quickly across the bathroom, grabbed her toothbrush off its hook and began brushing her teeth with it.

The dry brush tasted terrible, but before she could wet it or squeeze out some toothpaste, Mr. Berryfield came bounding up the cellar stairs. In the mirror over the sink, she saw him catch sight of her and stop dead.

"Jan! I didn't hear you. You're up early."

"Yes. I dreamed our mouse was racing in the tub again, so I came to see if it was true. But it wasn't. Daddy—" Janet faced her father, "do you think those cats drove him away for good?"

Mr. Berryfield blinked and hesitated. He couldn't truthfully say yes, and he didn't want to say no. Before he had to answer, Mrs. Berryfield arrived at the bathroom door with more questions.

"Arthur!" she exclaimed. "On a Saturday morning? How did you manage not to wake me? What have you been doing up so early?"

"Tinkering, Dorothea. Down in my shop, tinkering. I had some ideas about that mousetrap of mine, and couldn't sleep. It still needs one or two small adjustments."

It was a sunny late-April morning — too beautiful to stay indoors, yet Janet did want to look in that trap and see if the bicycle mouse was really there. It seemed that whenever she came in the house her father was down in his shop, standing beside the bench, looking at the trap in deep thought.

Janet didn't want him to know what she had overheard from the top of the cellar stairs before breakfast. It was best for him to believe his secret about the mouse was safe. She guessed he was only pretending to work on the trap so he could keep an eye on the mouse.

"Don't interrupt me," he told her once. "When I'm inventing, I don't like to be bothered."

After lunch, he picked up his new paperback mystery story in the living room, and Janet saw her chance. Whenever he got started in one of those books, he was stuck for at least an hour. She tiptoed down the cellar stairs, balancing a saucer of water for the mouse and half a piece of toast which she had saved in her pocket from breakfast. She approached the trap and lifted its cover with trembling fingers.

There was O Crispin, down on the wire-covered floor, sitting up on his haunches like a squirrel. His nose was buried almost to the eyes in a piece of cheese so big that he had to hug it with both front feet. Beside him lay a slice of white bread with most of its crust chewed off, and a dish of milk.

Who had brought him these things to eat? Mrs. Berry-

field couldn't have done it; she didn't know the mouse was there. Thinking back, Janet grew more and more certain that only her father had been in the cellar that morning. Could he be the one who had fed the mouse — the same mouse who had scratched his precious tub? Was it possible?

18

CR MR. BERRYFIELD KNEW very well who had fed the mouse. He had. But as he drank his coffee after supper that evening, he still wasn't sure why. Was he sorry for the little creature — being stupid enough to be caught in a baitless trap? Or was he grateful to be shown that his trap could work? Or what?

He had eaten supper in silence, as his thoughts circled around the question which had been nagging him all day: for some reason he had fed the mouse this morning and what was he going to do with him now?

It was the last thing in the world he could discuss with Mrs. Berryfield and Janet. They must not be allowed to know that their bicycle-mouse had escaped the pet shop cats and was now in the cellar workshop. He swished what was left of his coffee in the bottom of the cup, drank it, and put the cup down.

"What's on your mind, Jan?" he said. "You keep looking as if you were about to say something, but you haven't spoken a word all through supper."

"I haven't?" Janet tried hard to sound surprised. "I guess I was wondering, Daddy — if you found our mouse was still in the house, what would you do?"

"If I found—?" How did she happen to be asking that?

"If I found your mouse?" he repeated. "But, Jan, how could he still be here? What makes you ask? Have you seen him? Or heard him?"

"You wouldn't get those cats again? Would you, Daddy?"

Mr. Berryfield pushed back his chair. He picked a crumb from his lap and dropped it in his empty coffee cup. Then he folded his napkin and set it on the table. At last he said, "That would depend."

"What's that, Arthur?" said Mrs. Berryfield. "You said it would depend? On what?"

"Oh," replied Mr. Berryfield, getting to his feet. "It would depend on several things: if there really was a bicycle, for instance. Things like that."

"You mean," Janet persisted, "if there was a bicycle, you wouldn't?"

"Wouldn't what?" He frowned.

"Send for the cats again? Try to get rid of him?"

"Oh, it would depend on more than that, you know. Such as, is it true he scratched my tub? And if I took pity and decided not to get rid of him, would I come home some day and find you two had made him into a pet?" Mr. Berryfield threw up his hands. "A pet mouse! Racing around this place on a bicycle! Good Lord!"

It seemed to Mr. Berryfield that the evening was about ten hours longer than usual. He had made up his mind what to do with the mouse, but it couldn't be done until Janet was asleep for the night. And he preferred to wait until Mrs. Berryfield was asleep too. It would be easier if she never knew about it. He lay absolutely still in bed, listening and waiting.

The house grew so quiet that he could hear a dry leaf sliding on the walk outdoors. Not a sound came from Janet's room across the hall. Mrs. Berryfield had been breathing deeply and evenly for the last ten minutes.

He inched out of bed. Moonlight was reflected so strongly through the windows that he needed no other light to find his way to the cellar stairs. In a few moments, he had brought the seesaw trap up from the cellar and was carrying it out the front door, holding it carefully in both hands like a platter of Thanksgiving turkey.

The night was unusually mild for April, and he hoped

none of the neighbors would be out for a stroll. He didn't want to meet anyone, or even to be seen wandering alone in the moonlight at such a late hour, in pajamas and slippers — and carrying what he was carrying. He hurried down the path to the sycamore tree, which spread a patch of heavy shadow on the sidewalk. Here he was invisible, but it was still much too near home for what he planned to do.

He looked up and down the street. All the houses were dark. The cement sidewalk gleamed white in the moonlight, except where black islands of shade were cast by the trees that lined the street.

Holding the trap firmly against his chest, Mr. Berryfield dodged along the roadside from one shadow to the next, half walking, half running, almost to the end of the street. There he stopped in the shadow of a huge maple. Beyond it, there were no safe shadows; nothing but moonlight.

He put down the trap and paused to catch his breath. A light breeze rustled the leaves overhead and fluttered the legs of his pajamas. Although it was a warm breeze, he shivered.

Why was he taking such a risk for a mouse? How would he explain himself if someone came along and found him here, or if the people in the nearest house suddenly saw him from their windows and screamed?

He bent down, uncovered the trap, and peered in. Dark though it was under the tree, he could see the mouse lying beside his bicycle on the wire-covered floor of the trap. Could he be asleep? The cheese and milk were all gone, and the slice of bread had been nibbled to lacework. The mouse lay on his side, the bulging blue helmet on his head, and all that outlandish rigging still attached to his bandaged tail. How could he sleep, done up like that?

As Mr. Berryfield watched, the mouse stretched his hind legs, rolled over to his feet and stood up. A shaft of moonlight through the leaves touched the dome of the electric-blue crash helmet and made it gleam like a tiny balloon.

"Mouse," Mr. Berryfield murmured, "you don't know how lucky you are. I would gladly have killed the villain who ruined my tub. But I can't help feeling very friendly towards the bubble-head who got himself caught in my foolish trap. I was friendly enough this morning to smuggle food to you. And I'm friendly enough now to let you go."

O Crispin cocked his head sideways and stared up at the speaker with a bold, distrustful eye.

"Oh yes," nodded Mr. Berryfield, "I've heard that the mouse who scratched my tub rides a bike and has a bandaged tail. If you're that mouse, don't tell me! I don't want to hear about it. That all happened day before yesterday. Whatever mouse you were then —" Mr. Berryfield gently tilted the trap on its side — "today you have been my own very welcome guest. And that's the mouse I'm setting free!"

Mr. Berryfield stood back a little and waited for the mouse to climb down to the sidewalk and lift the bicycle after him. He wished the mouse would hurry. Once again he felt he had never looked so foolish as he must look now — standing out here on the sidewalk in his pajamas in the middle of the night, turning loose this weird-looking mouse.

O Crispin adjusted his helmet and mounted his bicycle. He had no intention of giving Mr. Berryfield time to change his mind. There was barely time enough, as it was, to get to

the State Racetrack where the Bicycle Rodeo would be held
tomorrow evening.

In an instant of panic, he realized it might already be past
midnight. In that case, the Rodeo was not tomorrow; it was
today!

He stood on the pedals and, without a glance backward,
sprinted off along the sidewalk towards the big gates of Bel-
Air Park.

Until that moment, Mr. Berryfield had never seen O Crispin ride. He stared after him in amazement. No wonder Janet

and Mrs. Berryfield had wanted to make the little racer into a pet!

"If I hadn't sworn to get rid of him," Mr. Berryfield thought sadly, "and if he hadn't spoiled my tub . . . Well, he's gone. It's too late now. And anyway, it was only a mouse!"

19

IT WAS FRIDAY NIGHT AGAIN in Bel-Air Park. Nearly a week had passed, and the moon that had shone so brightly the night Mr. Berryfield turned O Crispin loose was now only a sliver, beginning to disappear behind the branches of the trees.

If anyone, returning home late, had glanced down the hill towards Winchester, he would have seen only the street and bridge lights still burning to show that a city was there. Everything else was dark. A gentle breeze drifted among the houses of Bel-Air Park. It ruffled leaves, and swung the curtains at open windows softly to and fro.

O Crispin wheeled his bicycle off the path and leaned it against a tulip in front of the Berryfield house. He looked up at the bathroom addition, a shapeless two-story lump blacking out the stars.

Under the sycamore he sat down on the lawn and slipped

off his helmet. His bandaged tail rested lightly on the cool grass.

The new golden feather fastened to the front of the helmet looked by now as tired and crumpled as he felt. Had it been worth winning? In the excitement last Sunday it seemed so, but since then he hadn't slept one good sleep, and he had eaten too many good meals. There had been dinners, dinners, dinners, and traveling nearly every day since his victory in the State Bicycle Rodeo.

The new State Champion was in demand everywhere, and his popularity was doubled by the fact that he had won his triumph with a bandaged tail. Twelve cities wanted him to come and perform in exhibition races.

The weekly mouse magazine, *Gnaw,* printed a long article telling how the Champion had overcome his handicap and outraced every opponent. It even mentioned the accident to O Crispin's grandfather's tail, and the plucky efforts of old G Rufus to get it to curl properly again after his encounter with the mousetrap. "Courage Runs in the Family," the headline said.

Of course, everybody was asking how the Champion's tail had been hurt. Someone said he had had a blowout while racing to catch a train. Was that true? a reporter asked him. O Crispin smiled and said the story was reasonably correct;

yes, he had missed the drain, but he hadn't really been trying to catch it. The reporter noticed he said "drain," but supposed he had a cold, and asked no more questions.

It was just as well. O Crispin would rather have given up his championship badge and feather than have to admit he had gone Rolling Down to Rio in a new track without first making sure the course was clear. Even more, he didn't want all the mice in the state to know about Mr. Berryfield's tub.

Night and day, since winning the state championship, he had dreamed of escaping from the long speeches, the big dinners, the lumpy hotel beds — returning to that beautiful white track with the smoothly banked ends.

And now he was here! It was too bad that a house with such a beautiful racetrack had to have people in it too. Of course, the girl named Janet and her mother would be glad to see him again; he was sure of that. But what about the girl's father? That man was a puzzle. Think of those cats he had turned loose in the house!

"On the other hand," thought O Crispin, "when I was hungry enough to eat the grips off my handlebars, he brought me cheese and milk and bread. He did call me stupid, but then he called himself stupid too. Maybe he was pleased to find someone as stupid as himself! And then, just when I thought he was getting friendly, Bang! he put me out of the house!"

Perhaps he was one of those strange people who disapproved of bicycle races; or was it possible he had never seen one? Certainly he had never watched O Crispin practicing in the bathtub.

"If he could see me," the Champion thought; "if he could once see me riding on that best of all racetracks, I bet he'd be glad to have me stay in the house. And he would never again call me the stupidest mouse in Merrimack County."

Getting into the house was an all-night job. While O Crispin was away, Mr. Berryfield had discovered all the secret holes and plugged them solid, so the sun was high before O Crispin had gnawed a hole large enough to let him and his bicycle through into the cellar. He hadn't had to gnaw any wood for weeks and he found Mr. Berryfield's plugs took more chewing than fried chicken and eclairs. But at last he was in.

He hardly recognized the workshop. The floor had been swept and Mr. Berryfield's tools were all hung up against their shadow pictures on the wall. A box which looked very much like the seesaw trap was on the bench.

Luckily, the long board was still lying along the side of the stairs. O Crispin pushed his bicycle up it to the landing, where a crack of light showed that the door to the bathroom

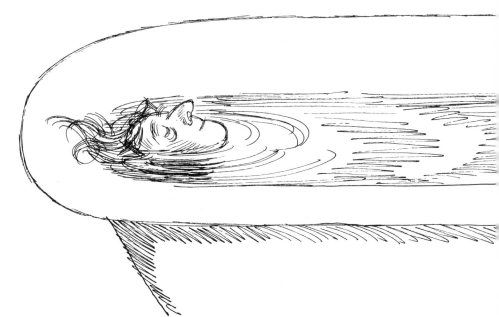

was not quite shut. He stood there, out of breath, listening.

Not a sound came from the room beyond. In another moment, he was safely through and had started up the towel rack legs.

This climb was even more tiring than the board on the stairs. But though he puffed and sweated and had to slow down more than once, his feet tingled as he thought of the hurtling figure eights he would soon be making in the smooth white track. Would Janet and her mother come and watch him? Perhaps, this time, Mr. Berryfield would be there too. He would find out who was stupid and who wasn't.

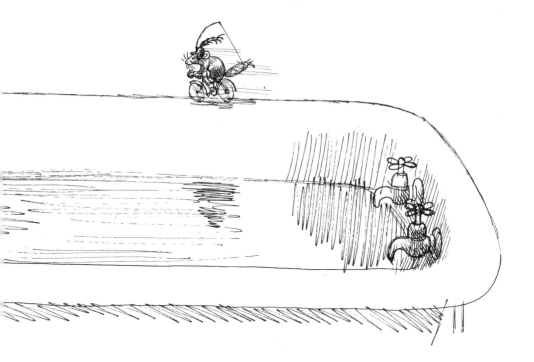

O Crispin arrived at last at the hinge in the rack where he could step over to the tub. He looked across.

Drat!

The tub was full of soapy water. Worse yet, Mr. Berryfield was in it. His head lay propped against one end and his chin was half submerged, so that the water came almost to his lips. He had shoved his glasses up on his forehead and shut his eyes. A serene smile glowed over his whole face.

As O Crispin watched, one of Mr. Berryfield's hands rose from the water and scratched his ear; then slipped out of sight again. His eyes stayed shut.

"Well," O Crispin thought to himself, "that settles that! No figure eights this morning! But since I'm here I'll work off some fat by taking a few turns around the edge. The man looks harmless enough. If he opens his eyes, he'll get a free show and I may win another friend."

In the week he had been away, O Crispin had forgotten how deliciously his tires rolled on the gleaming surface. It was smooth as cream. Each time he passed Mr. Berryfield's head, he had to steer carefully to avoid some long strands of the sleeper's hair that lay on the tub rim. Round and round he rode, at an easy, comfortable speed, until he knew the shapes and timing of the curves almost by heart.

He was wishing it were possible to go on like this and never stop when, to his horror, he caught himself swinging into a curve with his eyelids drooping.

"Yipes!" he muttered. "I'd better watch out. I've gotten fat and careless. These ovals are putting me to sleep." But in spite of himself, drowsiness kept returning.

And suddenly — he didn't know how, because his eyelids had sagged again — his front tire picked up the loose end of one of Mr. Berryfield's hairs. Just one, but that was enough. In an instant, it wound around the axle and was tweaked out of Mr. Berryfield's head.

20

"YOW!" yelled Mr. Berryfield.

One of his arms burst from the soapy water, raining it everywhere, and as he slapped a wet hand against the top of his head, the jolt sent his glasses flying.

He opened his eyes in time to get a blurred impression of the glasses sinking out of sight in the water. While he groped for them, something else caught his attention — an impossible thing. It seemed to be a mouse pedaling a bicycle around the far end of the tub, under the spouts.

The impossible thing came along the rim of the tub towards him. It really was a mouse and it really was a bicycle. Moreover, his own uprooted hair was flapping against the enamel at each turn of the front wheel.

By now he had found his glasses, dripping wet and slippery with soapy water. They would be no help at all. Holding them in his hand, he lay there and stared.

Most people, having such a perfect ringside seat, would have thought themselves lucky. But as O Crispin rode round and round, sometimes whizzing beside him like a blurry ghost, sometimes in sharp focus above his toes, and sometimes out of sight behind his head, Mr. Berryfield wondered if it would make any difference to have his glasses on, or if he would still feel bewitched. Round and round him went the bicycle, now clear, now blurred, now clear again, as if the mouse were wrapping him up in a web of invisible threads.

Was this the same bicycle-mouse he had found in his see-saw trap and put out on the street last Saturday night? If so, why and how had it come back? Suppose it should fall off on the floor or — worse — into the tub?

As he worried about this, the glasses slid out of his fingers and disappeared in the water for the second time. Why were they so confoundedly slippery?

Exploring the bottom of the tub in search of them, his hand unexpectedly touched something mushy and soft. Soap again! It must have fallen in while he was asleep, and that was why everything was so slippery. He would have to try once more to get a soap rack that would fit the old-fashioned shape of the tub. Mrs. Berryfield had said the scratch in the bottom was his own fault, because of a sliver of soap he had allowed to fall in. She said this bicycle-riding mouse had skidded on it.

"If pieces of soap keep falling in," she said, "sooner or later one of us will slip and break a leg."

While one of Mr. Berryfield's hands found the sunken glasses, the other chased and trapped the cake of soap — thin and soft and slippery. He didn't want to balance it on the edge, where it would only slide in again, or where the mouse would run right over it, so he sat up cautiously, leaned forward and perched it on the cold water handle.

To all this the mouse gave no heed, but continued to ride round and round.

"Well," whispered Mr. Berryfield, "you *are* a bold fellow. Doesn't anything frighten you?" He felt for the rubber plug, pulled it out of the drainhole and looped the chain over the spout. Slowly the soapy water settled, gurgling in the drain. Mr. Berryfield seized a chance to step over the side of the tub when the mouse was opposite; dried himself, and got dressed.

"Now, young fellow," he said, "how do you expect me to rinse and dry this genuine antique while you're doing a merry-go-round on the edge?"

"Rinse and dry it?" thought O Crispin. Splendid! He had been eyeing with displeasure the gray curds left in the bottom of the tub when the water ran out. If the man would really clean the track for him, maybe it was a good thing, after all, to have people living in the house!

So he stopped his bike at the top of the head-end slope and, while Mr. Berryfield washed out the tub and polished it dry with a towel, he unwound the hair from his front axle, tested his brake levers, and loosened the chin strap of his helmet one hole.

He had discovered that the strap made his jaw ache a little if he left it too long in one place without loosening or tightening it.

He bent forward until the nylon thread began to lift his splinted tail. He was ready.

Mr. Berryfield had finished with the tub, which now gleamed like a mirror. He sat back on his heels and admired it. If only that scratch could be repaired! Was this mouse really the one who had done it? Certainly he didn't look at all guilty now, or stupid either.

The mouse's head was held proudly up. He looked like a champion. And wasn't that a new decoration fastened to his electric-blue crash helmet — that dark blue rosette with a golden feather sprouting from it?

O Crispin had his foot on the pedal. Right and left he glanced. He squeezed the rubber bulb of his horn.

"Weet! Weet!" it yapped.

And before Mr. Berryfield guessed what was coming, O Crispin had shoved off and was coasting down the white slope, waving with one hand while he steered with the other.

Something went "Clunk!" inside Mr. Berryfield.

"I've got to stop him," he muttered. "The crazy mouse'll crash!" But his arms and legs felt as if they were locked in stone.

"Crash, will I?" chuckled O Crispin. Barely touching the brakes, he swung wide of the drain, bending his course into a figure eight, and came barreling back along the bottom of the tub. Three, four, five times, he traced these double-ended loops, with a growing speed that threw the bicycle higher each time it rounded the ends.

"Here," he exulted, as the plug flashed past his ear, "is where they separate the Sunday riders" — the plug went by again — "from the champions!"

But something was holding him back.

The ends of his loops wouldn't stretch out. He kept rising to the same level as before, and no higher. Try as he would, he couldn't make the wind in his ears sharpen its tune. His legs were heavy and hopeless, as if they might suddenly go limp like boiled spaghetti.

"I should have expected this," he told himself. "It's my

own fault, eating those big dinners, staying up to all hours! It was enough to ruin any champion. I ought to know better."

If only he could stop and rest — but not with Mr. Berryfield watching.

Even before winning the county championship, he had made it a rule never to look tired. No matter how he felt, no matter if he was ready to flop over the handlebars and let his ears hang down on his cheeks, he would never give up, but would hold his head and ears high until the race was over and the onlookers had gone home and he was alone again. Only then, if he still wanted to, would he rest.

Some racers put on a big show of how hard they were pedaling and how tired they were. Well, if they wanted to look pathetic and make the crowd pity them, they could have it. O Crispin wanted something else: admiration for his courage and endurance. He wanted onlookers to turn to their friends and say, "There's a real mouse for you!"

Going flop was all right for losers; not for the Champion!

Mr. Berryfield was becoming impatient.

"Bubble-head," he grumbled, "are you going to disappoint me? Is this all you can do? Just go back and forth?"

21

THERE WAS A HINT of warning in Mr. Berry-field's voice. It reminded O Crispin that he was not just practicing for pleasure. Not this time. If he couldn't make Mr. Berryfield cheer his performance, there would be no more riding in this greatest racetrack in the world. He was certain of that.

" 'Bubble-head' is right," he thought. "This is no time to dream about taking a rest. That Berryfield man believes I can only go back and forth. I'll show him!"

O Crispin's weary legs cranked the pedals into a storm of motion. As he flung his weight on them, every joint and sinew in his body ached, but he gritted his teeth and thought, "More! More!"

Faster, faster, faster, and still a little faster he went; looping up the slopes, then streaking along the floor of the tub, pulling out the ends of his champion eights like stretched elastic bands.

Zwing, whee! Zwang, whoo! Zwing, whee! Zwang, whoo! A little higher; a little faster. Just a little, just a little more to reach the rim!

Mr. Berryfield leaned on the side of the tub, awe-stricken at the look in the mouse's eye, the tight muscle at the corner of his jaw. He didn't dare interfere. Any attempt to stop the bicycle or catch it would bring disaster. And whatever the mouse was trying to do, Mr. Berryfield began to wish it would succeed.

"Go it, mouse!" he whispered. "Go it!"

Strength surged into O Crispin's legs. The bike rushed forward. The tune of the wind was rising.

"Heavens and earth!" exclaimed Mr. Berryfield. "What's happening to his tail?"

"My tail?" O Crispin's hands clenched. Had it come un-hooked? He could no longer feel the weight of it tugging at the fishing pole in his helmet, or on the strap under his chin. The whole bicycle felt light.

"Mouse!" gasped Mr. Berryfield. "Your tail! You're going so fast that it's lifting! You'll take off!"

So that was it! O Crispin knew now why he felt so light and free. His bandaged tail was no longer hanging from Doctor Potts's fishing line, a dead weight and a handicap. There was slack in the line — enough so he could turn his head for a split second and look.

What a sight! The beaver-tail bandage had lifted on the wind like a glider and was planing along, as easily as if it had no weight at all!

And the bike was gaining speed. Higher it swung on the turns, and faster it streaked along the straightaways. In spite of himself, Mr. Berryfield flinched a little each time it passed. What if the mouse should lose control and fly right out of the tub, bicycle and all?

But by the time the rider had zoomed away for the tenth

or twentieth time, Mr. Berryfield had relaxed and was pounding his fists for joy on the edge of the tub.

O Crispin felt the vibration all through the bicycle and up his back.

"Here goes!" he told himself. "Now I'll show what a champion can do!"

Once around, and dive along the straightaway; up and around and dive again; up, up and around! He left the plug chain shivering as he shot behind it and, before it had time to hang still, he was back again from the far end of the tub to start it shivering again.

"Go it! Go it! Go it!" whispered Mr. Berryfield.

"He thinks I can," the Champion said to himself. "All right, Crispin kid: do it!"

Down from the spouts he steamed into the straightaway, charged up the head slope in a long slicing curve, and was on the rim and sailing around it before Mr. Berryfield knew what was happening.

"You've DONE it!" yelled Mr. Berryfield, yanking his hands off the rim of the tub and out of O Crispin's way, just in time. "You've DONE it! Yay, mouse!"

Footsteps came running down the hall.

"Arthur! Arthur!" Mrs. Berryfield called to him through the closed bathroom door. "Did you want me?"

"Want you? What for? Did you think I was drowning?"

"No, but — I was opening the front door for some visitors, and I thought I heard you."

"Visitors? On Saturday morning?"

"I'm afraid so, and they're here to talk to you. Come as soon as you can."

Mr. Berryfield was at his wits' end. How could he leave the bathroom now? Who could tell what the mouse might do while he was away talking to the visitors? Could he hide him somewhere until they were gone, where Dorothea and Janet wouldn't find him, where he would stay safe till later?

Why not put him in the seesaw trap? What was safer than that?

Mr. Berryfield had been fast asleep when O Crispin climbed the legs of the towel rack, and he hadn't stopped to wonder how a mouse on a bicycle could get up on the edge of the tub. As far as he could see, there was no way for the mouse to leave it now. He wagged a forefinger at him.

"Bubble-head," he said, "wait for me there. I won't be long." And he disappeared down the cellar stairs.

O Crispin was alarmed by this odd behavior. What was the man up to, and was it wise to wait for him? But champions are used to making quick decisions in emergencies.

By the time Mr. Berryfield returned with the seesaw trap,

there was no sign of mouse or bicycle. It seemed impossible. Mr. Berryfield examined the tub inside and out. He looked for any new marks in the enamel to indicate a fall from the edge; he got down on hands and knees and looked behind the three lions' feet and the pile of paperbacks; he hunted all over the floor. But he found nothing.

"I just hope the bubble-head didn't go down the drain hole," he muttered. "But where else?"

He had no time to search any further. Mrs. Berryfield was knocking again, to remind him of the waiting visitors.

"I'm coming. I'm coming," he said. Shaking his head in perplexity, he left the trap on the floor by the tub and went out, carefully closing the door behind him.

22

NO CRISPIN HAD NOT gone down the drain. He had not fallen or disappeared. He wasn't really hiding. While Mr. Berryfield was searching for him, he was simply walking his bike down one of the scissor legs of the towel rack, and by good luck a towel had been hanging between him and Mr. Berryfield.

He reached the floor just as the bathroom door closed, and stopped to rest. Holding back the bicycle on that steep slope had made his legs ache.

How could Janet's father possibly think he might have gone down the drain on his bicycle? Not even Fritz would be so stupid!

"That Berryfield!" O Crispin muttered. "He's the most obstinate man I ever saw. He's made up his mind I must be a champion beetle-brain, and all because I walked into that seesaw box of his. Speaking of which — isn't this it, right here?"

O Crispin had caught sight of the homemade trap left behind by Mr. Berryfield. Only twice before, both times in the dark cellar, had he seen the outside of the trap. Here in the bathroom, by daylight, it looked somehow different, but this box was about the same size, and it had the same kind of door at one end.

"If it *is* my old hiding-place," he thought, "I will know by the looks of it inside."

He poked his nose in the door. It looked the same as ever. The gone-away cheese smell was still strong. After all the rich food he had been eating, it smelled like home. He wondered if there might be a few crumbs left.

There was no reason why an intelligent mouse, a State Rodeo Champion, shouldn't climb the seesaw and take a look. O Crispin knew exactly how far he could go before his weight would tip the seesaw. So why not?

The doorway seemed narrower than he remembered, much narrower. By bending over, tilting his helmet to keep the fishing rod from bumping, and pressing tight against his bicycle, he managed to squeeze through, and followed the smell of cheese up into the darkness.

"This time," he said to himself, "I know where to stop. It's when you stand up and reach for that shelf at the end — that's when the seesaw goes down. I won't do that again."

Fearlessly, he climbed the path until his nose touched the bottom of the shelf. The smell of gone-away cheese was so strong he could almost taste it!

His head swam — but not from the smell of cheese.

Down dropped the end of the seesaw too suddenly for him to back away. It plunked on the floor of the trap, and off rolled the astonished O Crispin with his bicycle, exactly as they had done before. As the seesaw returned to its place with a click, he didn't even look up. He lay there, face down, grinding his teeth and beating the wire-covered floor with his fists.

"Stupid! Stupid! Stupid! Fat and stupid! The seesaw's just the same, but I'm not. I should have known it by the tightness of that door. After all those big dinners, I must weigh as much as two mice. And I'm stupid enough for two!

"Fat and stupid, that's me! Champion Booby of Merrimack County!"

23

MR. BERRYFIELD FOUND HARRY, Silvester Pye, Bangs the Blacksmith, and the pale blue dentist, Doctor Norton, standing around the living room, grinning nervously, and with their hands behind their backs. Doctor Potts was there, too, fingering his stethoscope.

"Mr. Berryfield," began Doctor Norton, "we—" He became very red in the face. "Excuse me, Daddy Bangs, *you* were going to say it."

"Well, sir," said the blacksmith, rubbing his bald head but still keeping one hand out of sight, "we wanted to say—" He coughed and stared at the rug. "We wanted you to know — oh, hang it, Pye, you always did these things better than me. You tell him."

"Certainly, certainly," said Silvester Pye. "Glad to do it. Yes." He cocked an ear towards the sound of a clock striking in the hall. "Ten o'clock?" he said reflectively. "Now what was I supposed to be doing at ten A.M.?"

"Meeting us here, Uncle Silvester!" cried Harry. "That's what you had to do at ten A.M., and you've done it!"

Silvester Pye sighed with relief.

"Well, that *is* a load off my mind," he said. He didn't seem to notice that the others were waiting for him to go on, but smiled vaguely at them and added nothing.

"Uncle!" exclaimed Harry. "Aren't you going to tell the man why we're here?"

The old watchmaker opened and closed his mouth, frowned, and looked at Harry.

"Give me a hint," he said.

"Surprise—"

Mr. Pye brightened.

"Oh yes! A surprise for the Berryfields."

"For *Mr.* Berryfield."

"*Mr.* Berryfield?" Silvester Pye repeated. "*Mr.* Berryfield? No, it's no use. I'm stuck again."

Bangs the Blacksmith couldn't stand the suspense.

"Oh rats!" he exploded. "Here! It's for you!" He held out a clumsily wrapped parcel to Mr. Berryfield. "Careful!" he said. "It's heavy."

"Here's another," said Harry, bringing out from behind his back a larger package. "It's bigger, but much lighter."

Bewildered, Mr. Berryfield looked for an explanation to his wife and daughter, who had appeared in the doorway.

"But it's not my birthday," he said. "What are we celebrating?" The wild thought came to him that it might have something to do with the mouse.

By this time, Silvester Pye remembered that he too was holding a present behind his back. He tugged at Mr. Berryfield's sleeve.

"This is from me," he said, and put a very small package into his hand. "It's bigger than it looks."

Mr. Berryfield stood speechless. At last Harry broke the silence.

"Somebody has to explain," he said, "so I will. None of us four" — he made a sweeping motion of his arm to include the watchmaker, the blacksmith, and the dentist — "none of us really believed Jan here, when she asked for help to mend a mouse's bicycle. We thought it was just a story — same as you, Mr. Berryfield, when we said we came to your house to see a mouse ride a bike.

"Then we found out it was more than true. It was fantastic! Fry me a dodo's egg if it didn't turn out to be better than any circus you ever saw! A free circus, because it wasn't our house, or our mouse. It wasn't our bathtub that might get another gash in it. But it was no free circus for you! Yours was the tub that got scratched."

Harry paused, glanced at Janet, and then turned back to Mr. Berryfield.

"And when we heard that this amazing mouse had escaped the pet shop cats—"

"What?" snapped Mr. Berryfield. Did they know about his finding the mouse in the seesaw trap last Saturday? Had Janet heard him talking to the mouse that morning? Did they know he had also fed the prisoner, and let him go free? Mr. Berryfield scowled at Harry.

"Where did you hear that?

Harry fumbled for words.

"Well," he said, "I guess — I — somebody said — Isn't it true the cats never found him? That he got away safely?"

"How should I know if the cats found him?" Mr. Berryfield growled. "Maybe they did, maybe they didn't. If they did, they probably ate him wheels and all — if he really had a bicycle. Why should I care? Do you think I've gone soft-headed about a mouse, like the rest of you?"

"No," said Harry, "we don't think that, but — well, the

mouse put on a great show here last week, and you're the one who has to pay for it, although you didn't see it. We got our heads together and decided we wanted to show our—"

"Gratitude!" The word popped out of Silvester Pye's mouth as if it had just popped in and was too slippery to hold.

"So," Harry finished, "we brought you these gifts."

"Open them, Daddy!" said Janet. "Open them!"

Mr. Berryfield relaxed.

"All right," he said, "if you'll help me. I'm getting curious myself."

The blacksmith's package, as he had warned, was very heavy. Janet unwrapped it on the living room rug, and when the gift rolled out of its brown paper with a thud — a strangely shaped object, painted white — Mr. Berryfield had no idea what it could be.

He picked it up, felt the weight of it, and turned it this way and that. Suddenly, he knew.

"Dorothea!" he said. "Look!" He balanced it with one end on the floor. "Do you see now? It's a foot! An animal's foot made of — golly, it must be iron."

"Yup, iron she is," Bangs assured him.

"But whatever is it for?" puzzled Mrs. Berryfield.

"What's it *for?*" Mr. Berryfield almost shouted. "For my tub, of course! A real foot, to go where those paperbacks are.

Mr. Bangs, you're a prince! Where did you find this? Do you think it will fit?"

"Ought to. Made it myself. Try it and see."

Mr. Berryfield led the way to the bathroom. Until he came to the closed door, he had forgotten about the mouse possibly being loose inside, but by then it was too late to think of an excuse not to go in. He opened the door gradually. No mouse in sight!

While Bangs steadied the tub, Mr. Berryfield moved the deeply dented pile of paperbacks to one side and slid the new foot into place.

"Beautiful!" he said. "But isn't it different from the others? Those look like lions' feet. What's this one?"

"Mouse's foot," said Bangs proudly. "Because of that mouse with the heart of a lion!"

"And it fits perfectly." Mr. Berryfield stroked the new foot.

"I had a helper," said Bangs. He winked at Janet.

Harry's gift was opened next.

"Look!" Mr. Berryfield held it up. It was a wire rack to hang over the side of the tub. "To hold sponges."

"And soap," said Mrs. Berryfield. "Now nobody will leave a piece where it can fall into the tub to make bicycles skid."

The rack, too, fitted perfectly. Janet confessed that she had tested it for Harry when both her parents were out of the house, the same day that she had tried out the new foot for Bangs the Blacksmith. Harry had made the rack from a handlebar basket. Remembering how the mouse liked to ride around the rim of the tub, he had shaped the arms of the rack so they looped up in the center like croquet wickets and gave room enough for a mouse on a bicycle to pass freely underneath.

"In case he ever comes back," Harry murmured.

And what was in the tiny package brought by Silvester Pye? As Mr. Berryfield unwrapped it, the old watchmaker shyly said it might give more trouble than it would save.

It was a coiled clock spring with a hook on each end.

"See," Mr. Pye explained, "you hook one end over the water spout here, and the other end in the ring in the rubber drain plug, like this. Now, when you put the plug in the drain, the spring stretches — see! And when the plug is pulled out—"

With a "Twang!" the spring yanked the plug close up under the spouts, where it dangled out of the way.

"That will be safer," said Silvester Pye. "Don't you think so? When that mouse of yours was going round and round in the tub, I saw he could go behind the chain, but I kept thinking, 'If he runs into that plug, it will knock him cold.'"

Mr. Berryfield wondered if Silvester Pye's spring might unplug the bath some time while he was snoozing in it, but he kept this worry to himself. He stood back and gazed admiringly at the bathtub.

"It's gorgeous!" he said. "No one ever had such a tub before. Or such good friends. Of course," he added plaintively, "I *would* like to get rid of that scratch on the bottom. But a man can't have everything."

Doctor Norton cleared his throat.

"There's still another gift for your bathtub, Mr. Berryfield," he said. "You are lucky one of us is a dentist. Between you and me, this is a gift only a dentist could offer." He brought out from behind his back a small satchel — blue, to go with his coat.

"No," he said, when Mr. Berryfield reached to take it. "This is not the gift. This is my portable kit for house calls. If I could be left alone in this room for an hour, I think I could make you completely happy about your tub."

Leave him alone there? While the mouse was still hiding in the room? Mr. Berryfield hated to do it, but everyone else had gone out, so he followed them, pausing only to pick up the seesaw trap as he went.

"So you won't trip over it," he laughed, "and fall in the tub! Do be careful, won't you?"

24

"WHY DID YOU BRING that dusty thing into the living room?"

Mrs. Berryfield's eyes were fixed disapprovingly on the seesaw trap, which Mr. Berryfield had set beside his chair when he sat down. He had been idly drumming on the top with one hand. Now he picked up his hand and inspected the fingertips.

"Not so dusty as you think," he said. "Anyway, I can't put it back in the cellar till Doctor — Doctor — what's his name? the dentist fellow, lets us go through the bathroom again."

Janet glanced around the circle. They had been saying very little; just sitting and waiting for Doctor Norton's hour to go by. When Mr. Berryfield looked at his hand, Bangs the Blacksmith looked at his hands too, and began rubbing a huge thumb against the other palm. Silvester Pye had his head tilted on one side and was tapping a toe on the forget-me-not rug, in time with the ticking of the hall clock. Doctor Potts fidgeted, and now and then polished his stethoscope on one sleeve.

Harry grinned at Janet when her glance fell on him.

"What does your Dad keep in that odd-looking box?" he asked.

Mr. Berryfield was in no mood to talk about his unsuccessful invention.

"What?" he said. "Keep in this? Nothing. It's an empty box."

Mrs. Berryfield straightened her skirt over her knees.

"My husband is an inventor," she explained. "In his spare time. He has a shop in the cellar under the bathroom, where he makes things. Arthur, isn't this the mousetrap you invented? The one that didn't—?"

Mr. Berryfield bristled.

"Didn't work. Yes. But why mention it?" He turned to Harry. "They robbed it clean — the mice did — six nights in a row. Not my best invention!" He gave an embarrassed little laugh.

"That's nothing," responded Harry, "everybody fails sometimes."

"I suppose. Anyway, now you know why I rented the cats last week and got all those spring traps." Mr. Berryfield fell silent, looking gloomily down at the trap. But Harry wanted to know more.

"Then it never caught anything at all, this trap?" he asked. "I mean, later?"

"How could it?" snapped Mr. Berryfield. "If it caught nothing when it had bait, how could it when I'd stopped baiting it?"

"They say," Doctor Potts murmured, "that if a man were to make a better mousetrap, people would come from everywhere just to see it. They'd probably wear out his doormat! And his patience! So, unless you like lots of visitors, Arthur, you should be glad it's a failure!"

Silvester Pye pulled out his fat pocket watch.

"Half an hour to go," he sighed. He replaced the watch and settled his head on one side. His toe resumed its tapping, in time with the clock in the hall.

Bangs coughed.

"Might a hammer-and-tongs fellow like me see how that trap works?" he said.

Mr. Berryfield was wrapped up in his own thoughts.

"Arthur!" said Mrs. Berryfield. "I think Mr. Bangs wants you to demonstrate your trap."

"Me too," agreed Harry. "Give us a guided tour! Do we have to crawl through that hole to see what's inside?"

With one foot, Mr. Berryfield pushed the trap out onto the rug.

"Just lift off the top and look, if you like. I'm sick of it. There's not much to see."

O Crispin braced himself. Was he about to be discovered in the seesaw trap for the second time?

There was no shame in making a foolish mistake once; but to be caught making the same blunder again — that was a disgrace. Moreover, this time there would be a whole roomful of people looking on — the same people who had so admired the stunts he performed last week in Mr. Berryfield's tub. What would they think of him now? A fine champion he had turned out to be! Stupid, stupid, stupid!

Nowhere in the wire-lined trap could he hide. If he should crawl under the down end of the seesaw path, his beavertail bandage would stick out and they would find him easily. Better not hide at all. Better not even look up at them.

He heard the cover of the trap jiggle. Light streamed in. There was a gasp of surprise; then Janet's voice.

"Mom! Harry! Everybody! Look!"

O Crispin burned with shame.

"Stuff my pillow with potato chips!" he heard a man say. "Is this what you call an empty box?"

"Hooray!" exclaimed Mrs. Berryfield before Harry had finished. "It's our mouse! Our mouse, with his bicycle! I thought we'd never see him again."

Mr. Berryfield leaped out of his chair and looked into the trap.

"The scalawag! So that's where he went!"

Bangs the Blacksmith boomed in disbelief.

"You aren't telling me he's been in there all week? With nothing to eat! Look at him! He's as fat as a forge-rat!"

"No, I meant—" Mr. Berryfield's voice trailed off to silence. If they suspected he had seen the bicycle-mouse before, he mustn't admit he really had. "What's this he's got in here with him? Look, Jan, it's a bicycle! But don't try to tell me he can ride it! Not this mouse! Not a mouse stupid enough to be caught in a trap that has no bait!"

To O Crispin it felt like a bad dream, and yet he knew he was wide awake. He stood beside his bicycle, snapping the gear lever to and fro, not daring to look up at all the scornful eyes that must be watching him. If they wanted to name him Champion Booby of Merrimack County, he would deserve it.

"Arthur!" exclaimed Mrs. Berryfield. "Think of his feelings! Would you like to have a mouse talk about *you* that way? Besides, this is *our* mouse, the one who had the accident. Even after Doctor Potts bandaged his broken tail—"

"Dislocated," the doctor murmured.

"Even after that," went on Mrs. Berryfield, "he rode his bicycle with all the courage of a lion."

"So you told me," Mr. Berryfield remarked sourly. "You said he rode it in my tub. And you still talk about him as if he were a great hero. But if all this was true — IF — why is your super-mouse twiddling his toes now, in the stupidest trap ever made — a trap that wasn't even baited?"

"Buckle my belt behind!" broke in Harry, "if you haven't got everything backwards! How can you call a trap stupid which caught this incredible mouse? And his bicycle! And did it with nothing but the smell of last week's Limburger?"

Mr. Berryfield blinked. Was Harry joking? Did he really mean it? Did he think the seesaw trap was really pretty clever, after all?

"But what about the mice my trap didn't catch? The ones that stole the bait every night for a week?"

"Those mice!" said Harry with disdain. "Did you expect to catch cheese-wits like them in a trap as clever as this?"

Mr. Berryfield took the trap and sat down again, holding it on his knees. Janet moved over beside him.

"Harry's right, Daddy," she said. "If you had ever seen our mouse ride, you'd know he was something special. It takes a special trap to catch a special mouse."

Mr. Berryfield remembered the moonlit night when he had released the mouse on the sidewalk and watched him ride away. He thought of how, this very morning, the mouse had handled the complicated curves of the tub at breathtaking speed. He nodded slowly.

"That seesaw arrangement," he said, "did you all see how it works? Kind of tricky, don't you think?"

"Like the inside of a watch," said Silvester Pye.

"You should patent it," declared Bangs the Blacksmith. "People steal inventions like that."

"Oh — oh!" laughed Doctor Potts. "They'll be wearing out your doormat!"

Mr. Berryfield gazed admiringly into the trap.

"Did you put that clever rig on his tail, Potts? Maybe we could go into partnership, you and I, inventing things."

"Wonderful!" exclaimed the doctor. "Potts and Berryfield: Inventions."

"Or Berryfield and Potts," said Harry.

Over Mr. Berryfield's face spread the biggest smile Janet had seen there in weeks. He pulled the trap closer and observed the mouse.

"Well, you little rascal," he murmured. "They say I was wrong to call you stupid. You must be a clever one to get caught in this clever trap. I hope the tumble didn't hurt your tail."

"That reminds me," said Doctor Potts. "That bandage has been on long enough. If you'll help me, Janet—"

Janet picked O Crispin up and held him between her warm hands, with his head and tail sticking out. Doctor Potts had arranged the bandage in the beginning so that, after one small piece of adhesive tape was peeled back, the whole thing would slide off.

"It never was what I would call properly done up," he said. "Not really my kind of bandage at all. But it worked, didn't it?" Carefully, he pulled the fishing rod out of its socket on the electric-blue helmet. Janet was watching him closely.

"What's this?" she exclaimed. "In his helmet? Is it a feather? He didn't have that before. Is it something of ours, Mom?"

Mrs. Berryfield looked closer. Stuck in the front of the mouse's crash helmet was the long golden feather, which swept back like a wisp of sunlit smoke.

"It's not ours, no. I can't imagine where it came from. No member of our family ever had feathers like that."

"I mean, do you think he found it in our house?"

"In the attic, maybe?" Silvester Pye said helpfully.

"Not in our attic." Mrs. Berryfield looked sternly at the old watchmaker. "I'm sure of that. There is no junk up there. And if I can prevent it, there never will be."

"But Mom," protested Janet, "this isn't junk. Look! There's some kind of badge at the bottom of the feather. I'll bet he won it, racing!"

"Ah!" thought O Crispin to himself. "There's an intelligent girl! She knows how to use her eyes. And her head. Imagine anyone calling my state championship feather 'junk'!"

Mrs. Berryfield was peering at the helmet.

"You're right, Janet. It *is* a badge. But who would race with a mouse?"

"Other mice."

Mrs. Berryfield frowned.

"They'd need to have bicycles."

"Of course," Janet agreed.

"But," Mrs. Berryfield exclaimed, "be sensible, Janet! Mice don't *have* bicycles!"

Mr. Berryfield pointed into the seesaw trap.

"Why not, Dorothea?" he said. "This one does."

25

"DONE!"

Doctor Norton's pale blue figure was standing at the door. As they looked up, he closed his little satchel with a satisfied snap. Mr. Berryfield eyed him uneasily.

"What's done?" he said.

"Between you and me," said Doctor Norton, "that was a real challenge to my professional skill. Probably not one dentist in a hundred would have dared tackle a job of that size . . . well, not one in fifty! But then, enamel is my hobby. Come and see!"

It was miraculous! The gouge in the bottom of the tub was gone. Completely. Mr. Berryfield handed the seesaw trap to Janet and got down on his knees to look. Would it come off white on his fingers, like Janet's toothpaste? No, it didn't, not even when he rubbed hard where the scratch had been. Only when he put his head into the tub at one end, and looked towards the other end, could he see a tiny ripple in the white surface.

"Be careful, Arthur," begged Mrs. Berryfield. "You're twisted up like a pretzel. If that's the only way you can see where the scratch was, you don't ever need to look for it again."

Getting to his feet, Mr. Berryfield turned to the visitors.

"How can I thank you all?" he said. "Especially you, Doctor Norton? This is one of the happiest days of my life."

He stepped back and surveyed the bathtub. It was beautiful! With the soap rack and the new iron foot, and Mr. Pye's spring on the plug — and now with the scratch gone — it was better than ever.

But then Mr. Berryfield found himself thinking: "There is one thing that would make me happier: to see the mouse riding his bike in this tub again!" The others would laugh at him if they knew it; they would say that old death-on-pets Berryfield had gone soft and changed his mind.

"You know," he said hesitantly, "I can't really believe that mouse of yours ever rode his bicycle in this tub. Potts, did you put that weird rig on his tail just to make me believe the story?"

O Crispin's tail twitched.

"That Berryfield!" he grumbled to himself. "There's no

rhyme nor reason to him. First he's all smiles and common-sense; then he acts as if he'd never seen me riding in his racetrack — as if he didn't know anything at all!"

"Arthur," said Doctor Potts, "you are without a doubt the most exasperating man I ever knew. Do you think I would spend an hour wrapping and unwrapping tape on a *mouse's* tail, and then wrapping it up again, not to mention helping wheedle him down off an X-ray camera and into a shoebox with apple pie, just to make you believe your tub was scratched by his bicycle pedal?"

"That bandage was no make-believe," insisted Mrs. Berryfield. "His tail really was broken."

"Dislocated, ma'am!" Doctor Potts spoke sharply. "Dislocated, not broken."

Silvester Pye looked from one to the other.

"But I understood all his teeth had been shaken out," he said, "because of the cogs on the front wheel."

"No, no, Silvester," Bangs murmured. "Doctor Norton bit all the teeth off with pliers and filed them down smooth *before* the mouse rode it. Remember?"

"The teeth of the *wheel,* that is," explained the dentist. "His *own* teeth didn't fall out. They are perfectly sound and solid."

Mr. Berryfield waved his arms.

"Stop, stop!" he said. "Wheels, tails, teeth — I don't want

to hear another word of that nonsense. If this mouse of yours isn't a phony, if he can really ride a bicycle, let me see it — right now. For all I know, he could have won that feather playing hide and go seek."

O Crispin could stand no more. How much proof did this insulting man want, to believe that the wearer of the Golden Feather was a champion of champions?

Janet had put down the seesaw trap by the towel rack. The top was still off and there was nothing to prevent him from climbing up the wire-covered wall and out — nothing except the problem of how to take his bicycle with him.

"Well, pat the butt end of a billy goat!" exclaimed Harry, staring into the trap. "Look, Mr. Berryfield, what your 'phony' is doing now."

O Crispin was halfway up the wall of the trap. With two hind legs and one front leg he was climbing, and he held the bicycle dangling over his other front leg. At every fourth or fifth crosswire, he halted and hung on with all four feet, to catch his breath.

Having arrived at the top of the trap wall, he was thankful to find himself close beside the towel rack. A long stretch took him across from there to the second slope of its scissor legs. A few moments later, he and his bicycle were on the rim of the tub.

"So that's how he does it!" Mr. Berryfield blurted out. Mrs. Berryfield smiled at him.

"Are you beginning to believe he's been up there before?" she said.

"Not exactly, no." He wished he had held his tongue. "I was thinking of — something else. But look at that! He's really riding it! Look at him go through those hoops of yours,

will you, Mr. Jack-of-all-bicycles! Hey, mouse, you don't need to duck!"

O Crispin pedaled smoothly around the tub rim. It was true, there was plenty of room for his head as he went under the arms of the soap rack, but he ducked anyway, each time he came to them — partly because he couldn't help it and partly because he didn't feel like taking any advice from Mr. Berryfield.

This was his first ride since the bandage came off his tail, and he felt as light as the feather in his helmet. Four or five trips around the rim were enough for a warm-up.

He halted his bike at the head of the tub; checked his brake levers; waggled the front wheel; set his gear shift in high. Then he tugged the electric-blue helmet firmly onto his head, ears inside, and tightened the chin strap.

Standing there, aimed for the plug, he remembered the only other time he had done his Rolling Down to Rio in that track, when he had failed to check the course first and skidded on the cake of soap.

There were no such problems today. Mr. Berryfield had washed and polished the tub, and the blue dentist had filled the scratch with white enamel, smooth as glass.

"Oh no!" cried Mrs. Berryfield as she saw O Crispin preparing. "This again? I don't want to watch!"

The tone of her voice sent a chill through Mr. Berryfield. Was the mouse going to try some wilder stunt than any he had yet seen?

"What do you mean, Dorothea?"

The Champion paid no heed to their alarmed voices. He was already thinking of a full-speed swoop into the tub, free of bandages. He squeezed his horn twice, "Weet, Weet."

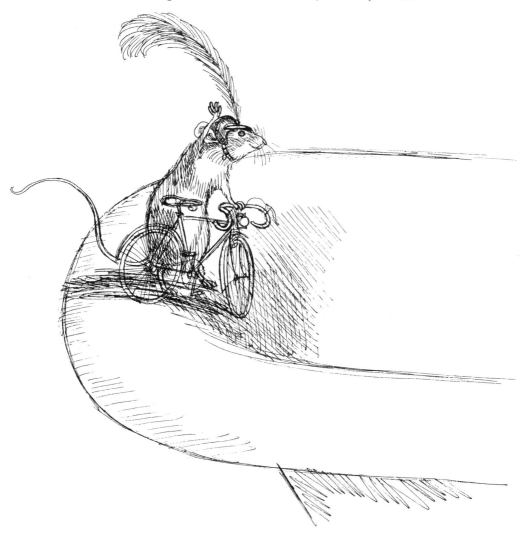

"Should we stop him?" gasped Mr. Berryfield.

But O Crispin had raised his hand in a champion's salute to his onlookers. He shoved off vigorously with his free leg, and plunged down the slope.

Janet's stomach felt like a huge empty cave. Her heart pounded. By now the bike was in the straightaway, O Crispin's tail flying like a streamer behind him. She saw his mouth open wide as he screamed, "Rio Grande!" but all she or any of them heard was the squeal of rubber as he clenched the brake levers; and the bicycle shuddered to a standstill at the very brink of the drain hole.

"Magnificent!" shouted Mr. Berryfield.

"I watched!" cried Mrs. Berryfield. "I saw it! I saw the whole thing! He was pedaling! He was going full speed!"

"And stopped in the nick of time," said Harry. "What control! What judgment! Put me to bed in a barberry bush if this isn't the greatest pet ever!"

"Pet, my eye!" said Mr. Berryfield. "This is a champion, that's what! Why didn't anybody tell me? What luck for us that he came to live in our house!"

"No, Daddy," said Janet. "It wasn't luck at all. Have you forgotten? This is the only house in Bel-Air Park that has—"

"A cellar!" broke in Mr. Berryfield.

"No, I meant it's the only one that has—"

"An attic! Is that it?"

"Come on, Daddy! You know what I mean!"

Mr. Berryfield frowned. Then a smile flashed over his face.

"A bathroom! A proper-size bathroom!"

"Warmer!"

Mr. Berryfield scratched his head. He looked all around. Finally, his eye lit on the bathtub. He rested a hand tenderly on its smooth, white, curving rim.

"Of course! A real—" He broke off, looking down at O Crispin, who had begun to weave a pattern of eights on the floor of the tub.

"A real racetrack!" Mr. Berryfield declared triumphantly. "That's what we have that no one else has. A racetrack fit for a champion!"

Bangs the Blacksmith had been examining the seesaw trap.

"You know," he observed, talking more to himself than to anyone in particular, "this'd be a dandy safe little house, if a man just made a few changes so a mouse could come and go when he pleased."

Mrs. Berryfield measured the trap with her eyes.

"We could glue a piece of old towel on the floor of it," she said, "to cover up those wires."

"Wall-to-wall carpet," said Silvester Pye.

"Maybe the mouse would hang his fishing rod and line on the wall, to remember me by," Doctor Potts suggested.

"There's lots of wall space," Janet pointed out, "to put up his racing prizes — things like that."

"Room for a bicycle too," said Harry, "under the seesaw."

Mr. Berryfield was still watching the mouse, as the figure eights grew longer and loopier and stretched further and further up the ends of the tub.

"I'll have to check," he murmured, "each evening before going to bed, to be sure nothing slippery or bumpy is in there to upset him."

"Daddy!" said Janet. "Do you really mean that?"

"There's no reason," Mr. Berryfield replied, "why it can't be a racetrack in the morning and a bathtub in the evening. But any more accidents would spoil it for both of us."

O Crispin was thinking his own thoughts.

He would always know, now, that champions have crack-ups — just like anybody — when they're careless and stupid. Yes, stupid! No matter what Harry said, it was plain stupidity to be caught twice in the same trap by nothing but the smell of gone-away cheese.

Of course, the trap had saved his life too.

"So I guess," he chuckled to himself, "I ought to be glad I was stupid!"

He remembered the crowded days of exhibition races, the long dinners and late nights. No more of that for him! What was the use of being Champion if it made you fat and short of breath? He would be a new kind of champion.

Already he was feeling more like himself. The bicycle rolled along like the wind.

"Once I get back in shape," he thought, "I could go on riding like this for a month without stopping to rest. My legs must have grown stronger than ever, carrying the weight of that beaver-tail bandage last week. And now I'm free of it! This really feels like flying!"

"Glory be!" he said to himself. "What are you waiting for, O Crispin? What is there to stop you from becoming Champion of the World?"

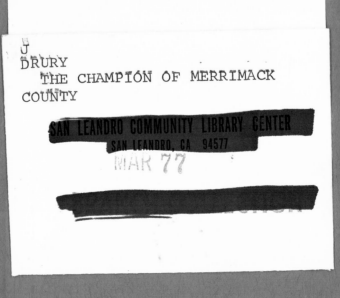